Ace Doubles

Eric Brown

Stone Owl Stories

They say science fiction ain't what it used to be. They're wrong. While Eric Brown is around, there will always be stories that pay homage to the SF traditions but bring a contemporary sensibility to the genre as well. His writing is elegant, elegiac and evocative, and proves that true style never goes out of date.

– James Lovegrove

Ace Doubles

Eric Brown

ISBN: 978-1-8381268-4-1

Stone Owl Stories

Series Editor: Andrew J. Wilson

Published by

Shoreline of Infinity

Edinburgh, Scotland

Cover illustration: Stephen Pickering

A catalogue record for this book is available from the British Library

If you enjoyed this book, find out more about what we do at

www.shorelineofinfinity.com

220421

For Finn and Freya

ONE

I was finishing the outline of a thriller set on Mars when the phone rang.

"Ed Bentley," I said.

"Ed, Charles here."

"Speak of the devil."

"Come again?"

"I was just thinking about you," I said. "I was wondering what the situation was with Danny at Worley and Greenwood. They've been sitting on the last outline for three months now."

"Ah..." my agent said.

One word, two letters, a prolonged aspiration. "Ah..." For all its brevity, it was freighted with the intimation of dire tidings.

"Go on," I said.

"That's what I'm phoning about."

"Bad news?"

"Well, not all bad news."

What the hell, I thought, did he mean by that?

"Let me guess," I said. "Danny wants the location switched from Britain to the US? He wants me to change the leading man to a leading lady – preferably a feisty, ass-kicking lesbian? And instead of the novel being SF, he wants some cute girl-meets-girl urban vampire romance shite. Am I close?"

"You're a very cynical man, Ed."

I laughed, or rather, tried to. "I've been in this business thirty-five years," I said. "What do you expect? Anyway," I went on, "what doesn't he like about the outline?"

He hesitated. "Danny emailed just now to say he doesn't want the novel, full stop. Hard sell in the US, he said."

"Doesn't want it?"

"I'm sorry. I've forwarded you his email."

I sat back, vacillating between anger and despair. I'd been banking on the signature advance to pay a few outstanding debts.

"Very well… Look, I've just finished outlining that idea I had for a high-tech thriller set on Mars. We were going to try it with Gollancz, but I suppose we could run it past Danny."

A silence from the other end. An ominous silence.

"Charles? Are you still there?"

A long sigh wended its way through the telephonic labyrinth from his sumptuous office in Kensington to my less-than-sumptuous two-bedroom Hackney terraced house. "I'm afraid Worley and Greenwood have decided to pull the plug."

"Pull the plug," I said. "I like your use of the euphemism."

"You have to admit, Ed, that sales have been rather poor of late. The last three titles have hardly shifted a couple of thousand each."

"So they don't want to see *anything* from me? Anything at all?"

"I'm sorry."

I nodded to myself. I've been in this business long enough to roll with the punches. I knew the cesspit I was climbing into right back at the beginning, and I was the last person to start complaining about the stink.

But it still hit me hard, even now, when ... count them ... my *third* publisher in ten years had decided to call it a day.

Now I managed to laugh. "I thought you said it wasn't *all* bad news?"

Charles brightened. "That's what I wanted to see you about."

"Don't tell me, Danny can offer me a job as a janitor? At least it'll pay more than what I'm earning now." I stopped.

Charles had said he wanted to see me. He very rarely wanted to *see* me.

"Something's come up," he went on. "It might be lucrative. Well, no 'might be' about it. It *will* be lucrative. Are you free for lunch?"

"At the Chandigarh?" I said.

"You're on."

"And the King's afterwards for a few jars?"

"Why not?" he said.

"So what's the deal?"

"Not now. We'll discuss it over lunch."

That was ominous. The deal was obviously something I'd refuse to touch point blank on the phone. I needed persuading over a curry and a few pints.

He changed the subject. "Anyway, how's the luscious Sula?"

How long had it been since I'd last spoken to my agent? Months, obviously. "She left me three months ago."

"Left you?" He sounded aghast. "But ... my boy – how are you?"

"I'm fine. More than fine. I'm over it. I feel..." I was about to say I was feeling "liberated", but that would be lying – although there were periods, between the despair, when I was beginning to enjoy my own company.

"Dare I venture to ask what happened?"

"What do you think? She met someone else. No doubt someone younger, fitter and richer."

He picked up on the "fitter".

"Ah, and how is the arthritis these days?"

You did ask, I thought.

"I now have the fucking thing in my spine, my right hip and left shoulder, both my knees and ankles, as well as everywhere else. And the methotrexate I'm taking to supposedly inhibit the sodding disease makes me ill three days a week."

He sighed. "Ed, Ed … the drinks are on me today, hmm?"

"And the meal," I said.

"See you at the Chandigarh at one."

*

And while I'm complaining, and drunk … Danny at Worley and Greenwood emailed, via my agent, bouncing the outline. One line stands out: "I'm not at all against SF set in Britain or Europe – but going forward, as our main market is the US, we must think about the advisability of using non-European settings in future…"

Hey-ho, so now we know. The Yanks are so fucking insular they can't take their SF not set in the US.

– Ed Bentley, in an email to Ian Whates

*

Back then, I spent a lot of time staring into space. I'd slip into a morass of despair, and mull over what had been and what might be, and I didn't know which was more frightening.

My study was my sanctuary. It contained many worlds that were not my own, and a few that were. These worlds were contained in small rectangles of processed timber called books, the fantasies of a thousand minds. They were my escape when I read them, and my escape when I wrote my own. My *escape* – I admit it. It's all very well for pseudo-intellectuals to spout high-flown nonsense about the deeper meaning of their oeuvre – but *I* wrote, *I* told stories, in order to escape the many exigencies of my existence. I lost myself in other worlds of my invention, and resurfaced, hours later, feeling refreshed, my futile life seemingly invested with some small purpose.

The pity is that this feeling never lasted for more than a day, like some wonderful but evanescent drug.

I left my desk and crossed to the shelves that spanned the length of the wall opposite the window. The eight planks of planed pine were ranked with over two thousand paperback science-fiction novels, collections and anthologies, ranging from Aldiss to Zelazny. The top shelf was given over to over three hundred Ace Doubles: two short novels in one volume, bound back-to-back but upside-down in relation to each other. The paper was ageing and sepia-coloured, and the typeface was fading, but the covers – fine work by the likes of Gaughan, Emshwiller, and Freas – were still as vibrant and evocative to me as they were when, as a naive teenager sequestered in far-away Australia in the seventies, I was drawn to the images of swooping starships and predatory aliens.

These were action-adventure novels by the likes of Robert Silverberg, E. C. Tubb and Philip E. High. I discovered Ace Doubles in the basement of a second-hand bookshop in Degraves Street, Melbourne, and the tales of intrigue and adventure on distant worlds allowed the lonely, homesick teenager brief respites from fear and anxiety. They changed my life; they made me what I am today, a man who escapes reality by spinning fantasies for others like himself.

I still read the occasional Ace Double, luxuriating in the sense of nostalgia that they evoke: the remembrance of who I used to be, as I tried to recapture that long-lost sense of wonder. They were a comfort, despite the often-hackneyed prose and cliched plots.

I pulled *Secret Agent of Terra* from the shelf, flicked through its pungent pages, and smiled as I read a line here and there. I admired the cover, depicting a woman spacer standing on a spur of rock high above an alien landscape, and I felt a little better.

I returned the John Brunner to the shelf and set off to meet my agent.

TWO

The **Chandigarh** is a small, down-at-heel Punjabi restaurant just off the King's Road. The owner is a rotund pygmy who goes by the wonderful title of Mr Jolly, and he has his priorities sorted out: he spends more money on his head chef and kitchen staff than on the furnishings and fixtures of his eatery. Consequently, the carpets are sticky, and the plush velveteen benches worn and stained, but the food is ambrosial. They cater for local Sikhs and the curry *cognoscenti* of the capital.

Charles was already ensconced in his favourite booth in the gloom of the restaurant's nether regions. Like the Chandigarh, he was worn and stained, and like the Chandigarh, he spent his money – his fifteen per cent fleeced from poor hacks like me – on food and drink. He had an almost empty pint glass of Cobra stationed beside the patched elbow of his corduroy jacket, and his attention was on the menu.

He beamed at me, a dubious benediction of nicotine-stained incisors and full lips. "Ed, you look well."

"It never ceases to amaze me," I said, "that my outward appearance bears absolutely no relation to the parlous state of my health."

I slipped into the seat opposite Charles, though I took up only a third of the space. My agent is huge. He's six foot four, and his corpulence when standing seems proportional to his height; but when he's seated, it tends to *spread*. His face is vast, red and multiple-chinned, and he wears his thinning ginger hair unfashionably long, compensating at the sides for what is missing on top.

"I'm sorry to hear that, my boy. Now, can I get you a beer?"

We dine perhaps once a year at the Chandigarh, and he never remembers. I'm something of a Puritan when it comes to curry and beer – never the two shall mix. I make up for this alcoholic abstemiousness in the pub afterwards.

He pointed a pudgy finger at me. "Don't remind me. For some strange reason, you prefer water with your nosh. Starters?"

I'm a creature of habit. "Mushroom pakora," I said, "and for main course, dhal paneer with three chapattis."

Mr Jolly waddled to our table bearing a pickle try and a plate of poppadoms. Beaming, he greeted us like long-lost brothers. We ordered, Charles selecting a chicken tikka starter followed by a keema vindaloo. "Oh, and another fine pint of Cobra, my man, and a jug of water."

I shattered a poppadom and shovelled it into the bowl of lime pickle. "Now, what's all this about a lucrative deal?" I said, chewing. "Who do I have to shoot?"

"Ha ha," Charles said, spitting bits of poppadom across the tablecloth. He took a great swallow of beer and wiped his lips on a napkin. "Business later, hmm?"

I ignored this and pointed a shard of poppadom at him. "A novelisation, right? One of those *Doctor Who* things?" I should be so lucky. Only the in-crowd landed those money-for-jam contracts.

"As I said, business later."

"Very well... But the situation at Worley and Greenwood – you really think the toilet is flushed and I'll never sell to them again?"

"You know what they're like now that the new fellow took the reins. They were bastards before, and they're even bigger bastards now. It's all about the bottom line, and artistic integrity be buggered."

I stared at him. Never before had I heard the phrase "artistic integrity" pass his lips. He lived by the bottom line.

"But I'm concerned for you, my boy," he said, changing the subject. "Your health, then all this business, and then you tell me that Ursula has left you..."

"Don't worry about me, Charles. I'm as tough as old boots."

"Are you and Ursula still on good terms?"

"I wouldn't know about that. Haven't seen her for about two months."

"Acrimonious?"

I thought about it. "No," I said. "No, it wasn't actually. She just moved out one morning and left me a note."

"Do you know who she'd met?"

"I must admit, I've no idea."

The starters arrived and I tucked into the succulent mushroom pakora.

Charles dabbed his lips with a napkin, eyeing me over the process. He has the large man's rather prim deliberation when it comes to matters of personal grooming, though the result was far from satisfactory: he left shreds of ginger on his lips and some unidentified ghee-like substance on his chin.

"I talked to Sally in the office when I got off the phone to you this morning," he said. "She knows everyone there is to know among the Chelsea set."

"Don't tell me," I said, only mildly interested. "She knows who's wooing Sula?"

"I do like your old-fashioned terminology, Ed. Wooing! And you accuse me of employing euphemisms."

"Out with it."

"Very well… It's Donald Tylesly."

I stared at him. "You're taking the piss?"

"Wish I were, old boy."

"Tylesly? That pretentious little creep?"

"He's bright, and a damned good editor."

"He's the bastard who wanted me to totally rewrite the third book of the *Orion Trilogy*, got miffed when I pointed out why he was wrong, and decided he didn't want to work with me again. In fact," I went on, warming to the theme, "I suspect it was Tylesly who got me dropped by Methuen all those years ago. And now he's fucking my wife!"

Charles murmured, "I think I prefer the term 'wooing'…"

I finished the pakora, took a long drink of water, then sat back and analysed my feelings. The odd thing was, my verbal protestations were no more than bluster – I was giving Charles what I thought he wanted to hear. The fact was that I really didn't give two hoots who was wooing Sula. Or fucking her, come to that. In fact, if I looked beyond my prejudice, I had to admit that she could have done a lot worse than someone like Tylesly, who at least was intelligent … despite being a creep.

I smiled when I realised that Sula would accuse me – and rightly so – of being apathetic.

*

I've just gone through my sales figures for the past ten years, and you won't believe this – or then again, perhaps you might. My best work, The Kings of Infinity, Tekani, The Quiet Invasion and the Yani books, all bombed in the marketplace. My bestseller, Spiral, which I knocked off in record time, has sold over fifty thousand copies to date.

– From an email sent by Ed Bentley to Keith Brooke, April 2015

*

The main course arrived, and for the next fifteen minutes, we lost ourselves in appreciation of our respective dishes and exchanged desultory shop-talk.

The dhal paneer was up to its usual high standards.

I wiped the plate clean with the last scrap of chapatti, sat back and belched. "That was bloody good," I said.

Charles fed the last few forkfuls of curry into his great maw, spilling mince down his shirt-front in the process.

I don't know what reminded me – maybe my fondling of the Ace Double that morning – but I recalled an outline I'd sent to Charles earlier that year. It was a personal project, aimed at a small US press that specialised in retro-SF: my idea had been for a short, forty-thousand-word space opera based on the characters created by the veteran English science fiction writer George Lattimer. He'd written more than twenty Ace Doubles in the fifties and early sixties, before following his editor Don Wollheim to DAW Books, where he'd penned another thirty or so titles until the mid-eighties. I'd read his 1958 *Voyage of the Intrepid* as an impressionable eighteen-year-old, and the story had stayed with me. My idea was to send his characters off on another galactic adventure, re-contacting the worlds that Earth had colonised centuries before. I was convinced that the US publisher would jump at it, but I wasn't expecting to get rich from the project.

Now Charles frowned as I reminded him. "Well, I sent your proposal and followed it up just the other week. My apologies – I meant to get back to you."

"They weren't interested?"

"Well, they didn't say that in so many words, but the editor I spoke to said there might be a problem."

"A problem?"

"The little matter of Lattimer still being alive."

I stared at him. "George Lattimer is still alive?" I was incredulous. "But … surely not? I mean, he was born around 1920, wasn't he? He must be 95 if a day."

"I looked into it. He's actually 97, alive and kicking and living in a little place called Allenby Wold in North Yorkshire."

"Well, I'll be…" I said. "He was a hero of mine when I was a teenager. Those time-travel police novels… I couldn't get enough of them." I stopped. "But I'm sure I read somewhere that he'd died a while back. I'm convinced."

Charles nodded. "Oddly enough, I was talking to Mike Ashley the other day, and I happened to mention Lattimer. Mike told me that there had been reports of Lattimer's death, five years ago. But they were mistaken. 'Rumours of my death have been greatly exaggerated…' et cetera."

"That's good to know," I said. "I wonder if he's still *compos mentis*? I don't suppose Mike knows?"

Charles shook his head. "He didn't say, old boy. Now," he said, finishing his third pint, "how about we repair to the King's for a bevy?"

"And this lucrative deal?" I reminded him.

"Over a pint, good sir," Charles said, yawing sideways and fishing in the constricted depths of his corduroy trousers for his wallet. "Now, let's see what the damage is…"

THREE

Charles had discovered the King's Arms by accident thirty years ago, the last stop on a mammoth pub crawl one riotously drunken New Year's Eve, and had insisted on dragging me to it shortly after I'd joined his agency.

The King's is one of those rare establishments that defies convention, and the worst efforts of the brewing trade to refurbish its holdings, and remains much as it must have been back in 1720 when it first opened its hallowed portals. I half expect highwaymen to be propping up the bar, and Hogarthian trollops to accost me on my way to the loo.

And the beer is Samuel Smith's; need I say more?

Ten minutes later, snug in a blackened oak booth with pints of foaming ale before us – extra stout in my instance, best bitter for Charles – I said, "Right, out with it? This putative lucrative deal?"

He attempted to repeat the line, but failed owing to the previously consumed pints of Cobra. "This putative ludicrous... This, this – never mind. Have you heard of Tuppy Cotton?"

I lowered my pint. "No. What is it? Sounds like a baby wipe."

He smiled. "It's a *she*," he explained.

"Ah, a porn star, perchance?"

"A YouTuber."

"What the hell," I said, "is a YouTuber?"

"I know you disdain all forms of social media, Ed, making you the only Luddite SF writer in Christendom, but *surely* you've heard of YouTube?"

"Vaguely," I allowed. "Something to do with online videos?"

"Something like that," he said, downing a good half of his pint. "Well, a YouTuber is someone who's big on YouTube."

"You live and learn. Anyway, who is Tuppy Cotton? Or rather, what does she do on YouTube?"

"She sings and plays the guitar – though I use the verbs with circumspection. The noise she produced can in no way, to my ears at least, be classified as music. Oh, and she writes."

"Writes?"

"Well, not really. But she thinks she does."

I sensed what was coming. "Go on."

Charles accounted for the second half of his pint and signalled to the bartender for a refill. One of the advantages of occupying his favourite booth in the snuggery is that it's within arm's reach of the bar. I finished my stout and took receipt of a second.

"She had a novel out a couple of years ago," he said. "A horror novel. *Night of the Blood Drinkers*, or some such."

I shook my head. "I'm not ghostwriting horror shlock for the hypertrophied ego of some adolescent YouTuber."

Charles waved me to silence. "Not horror, science fiction. She wants to write a SF novel."

I sat back, groaning. "Go on."

"First, a bit of back story," he said. "So a couple of years ago, Tuppy Cotton decided she wanted to write a novel. She'd been brought up on horror, and thought she could outdo King. So she tried, and submitted it to Greene and Golightly."

"It was dreadful, right?"

"It was worse than dreadful, Ed. Forty thousand words of ungrammatical, nonsensical garbage, according to Carmichael who worked there at the time."

"So what happened?"

"What do you think? An editor at G&G offered her a contract."

"Jesus wept."

"With the proviso," he went on, "that they get a writer in to 'tweak' the work. She agreed, pocketed a ten-grand advance—"

"But that's more than I've ever had for a sodding book!"

"And they got Guy Lincoln in to do the 'novelisation' of her manuscript. According to Guy, the deal was that he worked on the book at her place in the country. It was fine by him. He knocked it out in three weeks and pocketed three grand."

"Three grand? I thought you said this deal would be lucrative?"

"Hear me out… So anyway, Guy's paid the dosh and he's a happy chappy. The publisher is even happier when the paperback original shifts fifty thousand copies in the UK, and the foreign rights are sold to twenty territories. Then Tuppy Cotton signs a hardback deal in the US with Harper for a hundred thousand dollars. It goes on to sell fifty thousand in hardback alone, and double that in paperback."

"Christ," I said.

Charles shrugged his massive shoulders. "You have no conception of the popularity of these YouTubers. They're massive."

"Doing what, exactly?"

"In my opinion, sweet fuck all, but then what do I know? She sings a few songs, tells the world about her life, and now she's a best-selling author."

"And she's decided she wants to write a science fiction novel?"

"She told the bods at G&G, and they were falling over themselves to sign her up. She submitted thirty kay of clichéd space opera, and like the first time, the editor said they'd get someone in to 'clean it up'."

"So they asked if I'd like the honour? Christ, Charles, it's come to this – ghostwriting pure garbage for some teenage popsy… I could weep."

"Not a teenager, Ed. She's twenty-five, and the folk at G&G didn't ask for you – Tuppy Cotton did."

*

And the rumour on the grapevine is that mega-YouTuber Tuppy Cotton has just signed a two-album deal with EMI rumoured to be worth a cool million dollars!

– From the online magazine *Vibe!*

*

I lowered my pint and stared at him. "She's heard of me? On the grapevine, I take it? Heard I'm broke and desperate for work?"

"She's a big fan of yours, apparently. Read everything you've written. She wants to work with you."

I took a long drink of stout and considered what he'd told me. "And for knocking out this novel, working from her notes, I'd get *three* grand … while little Tuppy makes what, fifty thousand, more?"

Charles was smiling. "The three grand Guy got a few years ago was *before* G&G had any inkling how well she'd sell. Now they know. And working on projected sales, worldwide, they contacted me yesterday and offered a flat fee of twenty-five grand. Word length, eighty kay."

The highest advance I'd ever earned for a novel had been six thousand – now I was being offered over four times that to hack out an eighty-thousand-word space opera…

"Do you know what I feel like saying?"

He winced. "I can guess."

"I feel like saying I'm appalled that the industry has come to this, legitimising celebs who think they can write, traducing the genre I hold dear, and in general lowering the common denominator of literature – "

"Don't give me that sanctimonious bullshit, Ed!"

"But twenty-five sodding grand, for what … three- or four-weeks' work?"

Charles smiled with relief. "Attaboy! That's more like it. And twenty-five is G&G's *initial* offer. We have Tuppy on our side, remember? She *wants* you. I think that's worth another five grand. So … are you up for it?"

"I'll do it for twenty-five, but if you can get thirty…"

"Good man. I'll get on to Rob Riley at G&G right away. Oh, and Tuppy Cotton would like to meet you. Is it okay if I forward her your email address?"

"Go ahead."

"I'll get Riley to send you the thirty thousand words of 'notes', as he calls them, and get the contract sorted. And I take it you'll be free for a few weeks at some point over the next month or so? Tuppy Cotton was insistent that you work with her at her place."

"I'd rather work from home, if it's all the same."

"I'll see if there's wiggle room there, Ed, my man. One for the road?"

One turned to another four, in celebration, and at five o'clock I wended my way back to Hackney in a glorious state of inebriation.

FOUR

That evening, when I sobered up, I rang Guy Lincoln.
Guy is an acquaintance from way back; I see him at conventions every few years, and we share a pint or three while he regales me with the hell of his life. Guy is manic depressive: he writes when he's up and fights suicidal depression when he's down.

Evidently, tonight, I'd caught him in a trough.

"I've just finished the last of ten fucking westerns for Hubert and Shale. Ten of the bastards at a grand a pop. I ask you! Now I'm outlining a sodding Mills & Boon historical – trying to earn some serious dosh."

I sympathised, and wondered how to broach the subject of Tuppy Cotton without rubbing his nose in the fact that I'd be working with her.

"Guy … I heard you worked with a YouTuber called Tuppy Cotton a while back?"

"That's right. Nice kid, if a bit flaky. What about her?"

"Ah … nothing definite, but I might be ghostwriting a novel for her."

He took it well. "If you do, then insist on more than the measly three grand I got, okay? Hold out for ten."

"Thanks for the advice, I'll do that. But about working with her. How was it?"

"Piece of cake. We worked at her place up north. Hell of a pile. Ancient manor house in some old woodland near a village – and the local served a good pint."

"She let you get on with it?"

"In the mornings, we'd go through a chapter she'd written, and I'd spend the afternoon knocking out a couple of thousand words, expanding scenes, adding new ones."

"And her material?"

"Pure crap. She had a vague outline, a few half-baked characters with dubious motivations, and half an idea for a finale. But I'll give her this, she wasn't precious about her original conception. I'd butter her up with a bit of praise in the morning, suggest a few changes, then do my stuff in the afternoon. At five, before dinner, I'd read out what I'd written, and she was always happy enough with it. After dinner, I went off to the pub and got royally rat-arsed. Three weeks it took, seventy thousand words. At the time, I was happy with the dosh. Three grand. Ker-ching. Then I found out how well the fucking thing had sold. But beggars, et cetera…"

"You said she was flaky. In what way?"

"The usual mystical bullshit these kids get into. Crystals. Auras. Tarot. But when I told her I was a hard-line cynic, she dropped it. We got along okay."

"That's interesting. Thanks, Guy."

We swapped shop-talk for a while, then Guy said, "And remember, if you do sign on the dotted line, try to screw the bastards for all you can get, okay? Right, back to the sodding historical… Oh, do you know what Regency bucks used as johnnies back then?"

"I dread to think."

"The membrane of a pig's bladder. Imagine wrapping your cock in a pig's bladder before doing the business!"

"Bit of a passion killer," I said. "Thanks for that, Guy."

"Any time," he said, and signed off.

I was about to go online and search for Tuppy Cotton when the phone rang.

It was Charles.

"Just had an email from Riley at Greene and Golightly," he said, "and he's agreed my request for thirty thousand."

"Wonderful!" Thirty grand, minus Charles's commission, would pay off my debts, and keep me in curry and beer for a while.

"I tried to get it on signature and *delivery*, but they insist on signature and publication. You okay with that?"

"It's not a deal breaker."

"And there's no getting out of your working up at her place, unfortunately."

"I can live with that," I said, thinking that a few weeks in the sticks with a decent pub nearby might be just what I needed.

"Good man. I'll get back to Riley in the morning, and the contract will be forthcoming. Speak soon, Ed."

*

Tuppy Cotton's latest album reminds me, in its plangent romanticism and rejection of urban materialism, of the best work of Vashti Bunyan.

– Dan Gruber writing in the *NME*, May 2017

*

Later, I remembered my earlier decision to look up Tuppy Cotton. I returned to my study and typed her name and "YouTube" into Google.

She'd posted a couple of hundred videos, or whatever they were called, and I accessed the latest, broadcast just the day before. I skipped the ad as soon as I could, sat back and waited for the girl to appear.

She was not what I'd expected, which was some sassy latter-day punk with spiky hair, nose studs and attitude. The child that smiled out at me, from what looked like her bedroom, was small, fey and impossibly pretty, with a blonde pixie cut, a retroussé nose and a generous mouth. She looked a decade younger than her twenty-five years.

She was hugging her denim-clad legs as she stared into the camera, grinning. "Hi, there! It's a sunny day here in Yorkshire, England, and everyone's well. Say hi, Ralph, and hi, Nigel…" She reached out of shot, picked up first a big white rabbit and waved one of its paws at the camera, squeaking, "Hi there, folks!", and then a tortoise: "Hello," she said in a gruff baritone, which made me smile.

"I was thinking the other day," she went on in a light, well-modulated voice, "that I haven't sung you anything in absolutely ages, so this is a little piece I composed the other day called 'Sky Blue'…" She picked up her acoustic guitar, settled it on her lap, adjusted a tuning peg and smiled at the camera.

Then she began to sing.

I suppose this is as good a place as any to admit that I don't like music. I've shocked close friends with this admission, and made not-so-close friends consider me a philistine. The fact is that bad music does nothing for me, and good music – music I find moving and affecting – lodges in my brain and won't go away. My friend, the SF writer Tony Ballantyne, said that this is called an "earworm", to which I replied, "No, Tony, it's more like a mind-virus." I can't get the tune out of my head, and it doesn't allow me to think straight. It drives me mad, and the more I like a piece of music, the more it irritates me. Ravel's *Boléro* is like Chinese water torture, and passages from Delibe's *Lakmé* have been known to make me tear at my hair in frustration.

That's why, when Tuppy Cotton stared earnestly at the camera and strummed the first chord, I quickly reached for the mute key.

Only three minutes later, when she set aside her guitar, did I turn the sound on again.

"…hoped you liked that one," she said. "Now, some exciting news. You know a couple of years ago I wrote a book, a horror novel you all bought and said nice things about? Well, lately I've been feeling like writing another one. And you all know how much I love sci-fi, and I had an idea for this super space adventure about the crew of a starship that explores all these new alien worlds out there." She grinned. "Anyway, that's next up. I'm not going to say much more about it, but watch this space… And now, how about another little song? This one's called 'Lacey Sundays'…"

I closed down the PC, returned to the sitting room, and poured myself a stiff Scotch before going to bed.

FIVE

I rolled out of bed at nine, made myself a strong coffee, and was chewing a slice of toast when the phone rang. The pessimist in me wondered if it might be Charles, ringing to tell me that the deal was off.

It wasn't Charles – it was Sula, my ex-wife.

"Edward... And how are you this fine morning?"

I slumped into the nearest chair. I hadn't spoken to her for a couple of months, and I must admit that the sound of her voice made me feel as if a fist had reached into my gut and twisted.

"I'm well, Sula," I said. "What – ?" I began.

"What do I want? Is that what you were about to ask?"

"Well, something like that."

"What do you think I want?"

Sula had the habit, which had driven me to distraction in the latter stages of our marriage, of fending off my questions with ones of her own – and her questions were often asinine in the extreme, as was this one.

I said, with some acerbity, "I'm not a mind-reader, Sula. How could I possibly guess what you might be ringing about?"

"Oh, but I think you do."

"*What?*" I laughed. "Sula, you're talking in riddles. We haven't exchanged a word in months, and then you ring out of the blue and think I should know what it's all about."

"It's about," she returned, "your little friend."

"No," I said, staring out of the window at passing traffic. "Sorry. You've lost me. I give in."

"Your girlfriend. I forget what she called herself. Tippy? Toppy? Some ridiculous name like that."

I shook my head, confused. "What the hell…?"

"Oh, come on, Edward, don't play dumb. Your little girlfriend approached me at a party last night, introduced herself and started quizzing me about you." She hesitated. "Edward, I don't know what you think you're doing, but I'd be careful if I were you. She didn't look a day over fourteen."

"She's twenty-five," I said before I could stop myself.

"Anyway, she sounded besotted, wanted to know all about you. She said she was a good 'friend', ha ha, but it was strange… All her questions – as if she didn't really know you at all. And another thing that struck me as odd, Edward, was why someone as young and pretty as her should go for someone – and I hope you don't take this the wrong way, dear – someone like you, overweight, ugly and pushing sixty. Why, you're old enough to be her grandfather."

"Thank you for that," I said, "but I'm well aware how old I am. And let me assure you that there's nothing going on between us. She's an acquaintance, a business acquaintance. She works in publishing…" Which, when I thought about it later, was not exactly an untruth.

"Well, if she isn't a lover, dear, you have yourself a little stalker. But do me a favour, Edward, the next time you see her: please tell her never to bother me again, *comprenez-moi?*"

And before I could reply, she rang off.

*

Not only does Ed Bentley tell a rattling good tale in his latest novel, The Kings of Infinity, *but he makes the reader care about his characters. Bentley's logical positivism is a welcome antidote to the current trend of doom and gloom.*

   – From James Lovegrove's *Financial Times* review of *The Kings of Infinity*, Worley and Greenwood, 2008

*

I was in my study a little later, going through the Martian outline one last time, when I saw that I had something in my email inbox.

It was from Rob Riley at Greene and Golightly:

Hi Ed,

   Great to have you on board. I've just whizzed the contract to Charles, and here are Tuppy's notes on the novel.

   Looking forward to working with you on this!

   Best, Rob.

I replied to thank him, then opened the attachment, and began reading:

Chapter One

Wearily, Captain Marshall stepped from the hatch of the towering needle of the Intrepid and carefully stared around him at the desiccated sands of the equatorial veldt of Procyon III. In the silver, shimmering distance, a range of high purple mountains spanned the horizon like a graph denoting the fluctuating status of his recent mood: all in all he was having a very hard time with certain members of his crew, and then his bosses, the dreaded powers-that-be at Galactic

33

Exploration, had just landed him with a mission out here in the back of beyond.

He sensed someone at his side and turned to see the lovely Mila Sanchez smiling up at him. "Preliminary report ready, Captain," she said briskly. She nodded seriously towards the shimmering horizon. "Telemetry suggests that the crash-landed alien ship is somewhere out there."

"Very good," he replied promptly. "Prepare the team, Mila, and we'll set off. Oh, and break out the lasers. Who knows what we're likely to come across out there..."

I read on, drawn into the story as the resourceful Captain Marshall led his team into a hazardous encounter with the tentacled extraterrestrials of Altair V, aware that there was a traitor amongst his crew and finding that the aliens – far from being the bellicose warriors he'd been expecting – were surprisingly peaceable. Too peaceable by half, he thought...

It was hackneyed, poorly written, and feebly plotted – and several dramatic episodes failed to deliver their potential. And the denouement didn't work at all.

But ... it wasn't the complete rubbish that Charles had led me to expect. There was a certain naive charm to the story, the characters, and the approach to the planetary adventure. In fact, it reminded me of the kind of thing I'd read and enjoyed in my youth. It wouldn't have been out of place between the covers of an Ace Double paperback, circa 1955.

I could see ways of expanding the story, deepening the themes – treason and jealousy amongst the crew of the *Intrepid* – adding a sub-plot set back at the HQ of Galactic Exploration, fixing the denouement with a triple finale and a neat twist, and turning in a readable piece of action-adventure SF.

In fact, the work would be a piece of cake.

I was considering Sula's phone call, and wondering why the hell Tuppy Cotton had approached my wife at the party last night, when I noticed I had another email:

Ed, Contract from G&G attached. If you'd print off two copies, sign them and get one back to me. Good stuff.
   Charles.

I responded, *Will do*, printed the contracts, scribbled my moniker, then found an envelope and walked around the corner to the post office.

On the way back, I decided to reward myself with lunch and a couple of pints at the Coach and Horses. It was a wonderfully sunny day in early July, my aches and pains were at a low ebb, and I'd just landed myself a bloody decent book deal.

I sat in the beer garden, enjoyed a pint of Hobgoblin and a ploughman's, and wondered if life could get any better. Granted, my phone encounter with Sula that morning had knocked me off my stride, but all in all, I thought I'd coped with it pretty well.

I recall the first couple of weeks after she'd left me, the despair and the grief, or what seemed like grief at the time: the realisation of loss, of opportunities missed and – I'll be honest – the sickening blow to my ego at knowing that my wife no longer felt anything for me, but loved someone else. I'd wondered if I should have seen it coming, but after twenty-five years of marriage, it's easy to be anaesthetised by routine and complacency. You assume, lazily, that your own acceptance of a relationship low on passion and the torrid love that had first sustained it is mirrored by your spouse. And therein lies the fatal flaw.

Sula was *not* that complacent, and had sought another.

I had a second pint and, since that slipped down so well, a third.

I contemplated what Sula had told me about meeting Tuppy at the party, and after three pints, the encounter didn't seem that odd. Another guest must have mentioned to Tuppy that Sula was my estranged wife, and as Tuppy was – according to Charles

– a fan of my work, it was quite natural that she should ask about me, especially as it was on the cards that we might work together.

I had a fourth pint and made my slow way home.

*

Ed,

I'm leaving. I've had enough – last night was the end. I know I've threatened this before, but this time I've made up my mind. I'm staying with a friend; you don't know her, so don't try to find me. And no, we can't "talk about it". Don't you realise that the main reason I'm leaving is your inability to communicate?

Looking back, perhaps things would have been different if Ella had survived. But there you are.

Ursula.

– Note from Ursula Williams to Ed Bentley, 1 April 2018

*

I turned the corner into my street and saw the sleek, canary-coloured Porsche in the parking space outside my house. I don't drive, and I've bequeathed the space to my neighbours, a two-car family. I was wondering if they'd suddenly come into money and splashed out on the Porsche when the car door opened and a young woman jumped out and strode across the pavement.

She skipped up the steps to my front door and pressed the bell.

I came to the bottom of the steps and stared up at her. She wore light blue Converse pumps, tight faded denim jeans, and a jade-green T-shirt. Her hair was cut pixie-style, with faint green highlights.

It was Tuppy Cotton.

I called out, "Hello there."

She turned, smiling radiantly. Something I hadn't noticed last night on the computer screen: she had perfect, pearly teeth.

"Oh," she said, staring at me. "Ed Bentley? You don't…"

I smiled, and finished for her, "I don't look anything like my publicity photograph. Don't tell me. It's not recent – a dozen years old, as a matter of fact. Call it vanity. Or laziness. I eschew the promulgation of my image."

"Could I take a selfie of us?"

"I have never in my life," I said, "posed for what is termed a 'selfie', and I have no desire to start now. I take it you're…" I felt an odd reluctance to say her name, "Tuppy?"

She beamed and held out a tiny hand.

I climbed the steps and took it in my sweaty paw.

In her other hand, she held a mobile phone; I wondered if it ever left her possession. People these days seem grafted to the things, accoutrements as psychological as they are physical.

She gestured with it.

"I did email you, but you didn't reply."

I fumbled with the door key. "I've been out. The pub. Celebrating."

"You don't check your emails?"

"I do, but only at home. Twice a day. At eight-thirty before I start work, and again at four when I finish." This was not strictly true, but I am overcome with the compulsion, when in the company of the tech-savvy and youngsters, to play the old fart.

"That's … fascinating," she said.

I opened the door and bade her enter before me. "Fascinating?"

"I mean, what if you miss something important?"

I led her through to the kitchen and put the kettle on. "Believe it or not … Tuppy … I lived for many years without the beneficence of emails. Truth to tell, for much of the time I didn't even have a phone. I communicated by letter, hard though that might be to fathom. Tea?"

She shook her head in wonder. "Do you have green tea?"

"I do." I found the tea bags; Earl Grey for myself.

"For a sci-fi writer, Ed, you're terribly old-fashioned, if you don't mind me saying."

I winced. "Please, not 'sci-fi'. It's SF, okay? As a will-be SF writer yourself, you'd better remember that when you attend all those conventions."

She looked at me. Her eyes were huge and green, and I found myself wishing I were forty years younger.

"Why don't you have a mobile?"

"Ah, but how do you know that I don't?"

She nipped her bottom lip between perfect teeth. "I was at a party last night. Someone I know from publishing introduced me to your ex, Ursula, and we got talking." She shrugged. "Anyway, she went on about what a Luddite you are." She smiled as she accepted her mug. "It just struck me as odd that someone who wrote sci- – SF – should be so…" And she shrugged again.

We sat down at the kitchen table and I thought about it.

"I'll let you into a secret, Tuppy…" I nearly called her Little Tuppy, but stopped myself just in time. "A great motivating factor in my psychological make-up is apathy and laziness. I mask this with a front of sanctimonious superiority. I claim to disdain the craze for social media, mobile phones and iPods and whatever the hell, because of some well-thought-out philosophical opposition to the herd mentality, a railing against the idea of capitalistic excess that force-feeds us commodities we don't really need… But the simple fact is that I'm just too lazy and fossilised in my ways to embrace the new, to try harder."

She looked at me. She tipped her head to one side. "Is that," she said, "why you write the kind of SF you do, Ed – what some critics might term … good second-rate science fiction?"

Touché.

*

Ed Bentley's work has a firm grasp on the genre's tropes and a facile ability with storyline. His latest novel places him firmly in the second division of current British SF writers.

– From Susan Manning's *Foundation* review of Ed Bentley's *Martian Equatorial*, Gollancz, 2003

*

Writing this months after the event, I've inserted a scene break here in order to give myself a little time to think.

I had no idea that I was going to write the above dialogue with Tuppy – I had every intention of leaving it out – but the desire to set everything down, warts and all, prevailed.

You'll gather that, despite my somewhat patronising – some might even say sexist – depiction of Tuppy Cotton so far, she was as bright as a button.

This disturbed me, I admit. Not so much that she was almost thirty-five years my junior, and a woman, and far brighter than me … but that what she said forced me to confront some truths about myself. Or perhaps I'm lying in my denial that I was disturbed about her womanhood, and youth, and intellectual superiority.

I am an unreliable narrator, especially suspect when it comes to explicating the vagaries of my own psyche.

But to continue with the interrupted scene…

I suggested we move through to more comfortable chairs in the sitting room, and we carried out teas from the kitchen.

She kicked off her pumps and curled up on the settee. She was barefoot, and her toes were as perfect as her teeth. I couldn't help staring at them, and contrasting her perfection with the raddled state of my own body.

Every minute or so, her phone made a noise – are these devices designed to emit the most fatuous din imaginable? – and she attended to it with covert glances, complicit smiles when she read text messages, quickly followed by swift arpeggios of her thumbs.

When her phone made its facile clarion call for perhaps the twentieth time, I allowed her to reply, then said, "Can I see that, please?"

Frowning, she passed the phone to me.

I rose from the armchair, moved into the kitchen, and placed the offending device on the table. Then I returned to the sitting room and closed the door behind me.

"If you don't mind, I'd like to talk without being interrupted."

She looked uncomfortable, as if I'd violated her human rights.

I smiled at her. "Now, how did you find out where I lived?"

"Oh, that was Toby, the guy at the party last night. He works for Orbit, and he said you lived in Hackney, near the church. So this morning I asked at the Nisa on the corner if they knew where the writer Ed Bentley lives."

She fidgeted. More than once she reached out, a galvanic twitch, for the comfort of her mobile phone, only to recall its absence and wince. "I did try emailing you, as I said."

"That's okay. So, Tuppy, what else did Sula have to say about me last night?"

She scrunched her perfect little toes into the settee cushion. "Well ... she was a little drunk – "

"You're excusing her garrulousness."

"No, I think I'm explaining her honesty." She took a mouthful of green tea, not looking at me. "I wanted to know more about your work, your writing methods, your work habits. These things fascinate me, you see."

"Even though you think my work second-rate?"

"I never actually said that," she replied. "And anyway, second-rate is still very good, in my opinion."

"Go on."

"But Ursula didn't seem to want to talk about your books – other than to say that you didn't make enough money."

"She never read my work," I said. "She just complained about my contribution to the joint bank account. Or lack of."

"She wasn't interested at all?"

"What you must understand about Sula," I said, "is that she's an intellectual and artistic snob. She abhors popular culture. It's the circles she moves in, the damned Kensington gallery she co-runs. Fine art is her thing, and 'trashy SF', as she'd call it, doesn't get a look in."

"Doesn't she appreciate that popular genres contribute to our understanding of contemporary culture?"

Oh, I could have kissed her!

"Or perhaps she's blinkered," I said, "by the fact that she was married to a fat, apathetic slob for twenty-five years."

Tuppy smiled.

"What?" I said.

"She did say that one of the reasons she left you was because you were lazy and wouldn't talk to her."

I waved. "We did talk, but not about what she was interested in. Art, artists... And she couldn't give a damn about SF. Look, I have nothing against Sula. We were very happy for many years, but we just grew apart. And..." I was gabbling. The four pints were catching up.

Beyond the stripped pine of the kitchen door, her phone summoned, and her right hand made a Pavlovian twitch towards the arm of the sofa.

"Anyway, did you want to talk to me about something specific today?"

She hugged her mug and stared at me over the rim. "I was wondering what you thought of the novel... You did receive it, didn't you?"

"And read it this morning."

"And?"

I said, "I think we can produce a very readable book..." And I went on to tell her what I liked about the manuscript as it stood, and what she had done well. It was obvious that she had read a lot of SF, that she had a handle on the tropes, and a good grasp of the nomenclature.

But she was mature enough not to need her ego massaging, and asked me what I *didn't* like about the MS.

I pulled no punches, and told her that the plot was a mess, certain scenes undeveloped, and the ending disappointing.

She nodded. "You know, when I was writing the book, I kind of knew what was wrong, but thank you for being honest. I'm looking forward to working with you."

"And I'm looking forward to working with you, Tuppy."

"Ah… There is one thing. Would you call me Penny? I prefer that."

"Of course. Actually, Penny suits you better. But why call yourself Tuppy on YouTube?"

She regarded me, then said, "My parents christened me Tuppence, and called me Tuppy. It was just the first time they were cruel to me. So … when I started my vids, and singing, I decided to call myself Tuppy, and turn it against them. That way I win, you see?"

"You're not close to your parents?"

"You could say that. They live in Manchester. I never see them."

Manchester… I thought I'd caught the occasional lengthening vowel sound in her accent. "Is that where you have your house?"

"God, no! I couldn't live back there. I have a place in Yorkshire, way out in the country."

I sipped my tea. "About that," I said. "Look … is it absolutely necessary that we work up there? Only, I'm a creature of habit, and I have my routines…"

She smiled across at me. "Ed, I'd really like to show you my place, the countryside. It's idyllic, and quiet. And from the little I know about you, you need shaking out of your routines and complacency, I think."

I smiled. "Thank you for that, Penny."

"We could drive up in my car on Saturday morning, if that's not too soon?"

It was Wednesday now. "That's fine," I said. "I have a couple of things I need to tidy up before then."

"Great. I'll pick you up around ten?" She drained her cup and held it out. "Could I have another one, please? And then I'd like to ask you about some of your books, and have a look at your study."

Smiling – there is no flattery greater than that of a pretty young woman asking an old man about his novels – I repaired to the kitchen and made two more mugs of tea.

We'll end the scene there, shall we?

SIX

I **was packed and waiting** on Saturday morning when Penny
pulled up and automatically opened the boot. I stowed my
suitcase, opened the passenger door, and stared down at the
bucket seat in dismay.

"Ed?"

"I'm not sure I'm the right shape to accomplish this feat of
callisthenics without doing myself a grievous mischief!"

"Grip the top of the door with your left hand," she said, "and
rest your right forearm on the roof. Then lift your right foot into
the footwell, followed by your left. Now ease your body down
into the seat."

"All very well in theory, but in practise... Bloody hell!"

I dropped into the seat, breathless; my knees throbbed in
arthritic protest. I slammed the door, strapped myself into the
ridiculous confines, and we were off.

"It feels," I said, "more like being in the cockpit of a fighter jet
than an automobile. And need you drive so bloody fast?"

"Have faith in me. You don't drive, do you?"

"How do you know?"

"Oh, there's lots I know about you," she laughed.

"No, I don't drive, and I don't like cars. Infernal contraptions."

"You're a very odd man, Ed."

"I'll take that as a compliment."

She smiled. "I read the recent piece on your website."

"Ah… 'Fucked Over, Buggered, and Shat Upon – the Life of a Freelance Writer'." I glanced at her. "What did you think?"

She pursed her lips. "You paint a bleak picture."

"We live, my child, in a post-literate world of barbarians and charlatans, and these people seem to have taken over the marketing and acquisition departments of modern publishers."

"You exaggerate, surely?"

I grimaced. "Well, maybe just a little, for effect," I allowed.

She peered into the rear-view mirror once or twice as we motored at speed from the sunlit purlieus of Hackney and headed north.

I glanced at her. "Good God," I said.

"What?"

"You have a tattoo on your left cheek. I didn't notice it before."

"That's because it wasn't there when we met. It's a transfer."

"A transfer?" I peered at the thing. It looked like a letter from an alphabet I didn't recognise. "Why are you wearing it?"

"Because it's Saturday."

"That," I said, "explains everything. What is it, by the way?"

"A rune. Sowilō. It means 'Sun'. I wear a different letter every Saturday."

I looked at her, long and hard. "*Why?*" I asked at last.

She grinned at me, then glanced somewhat nervously, I thought, into the mirror again. "It brings good luck," she said. "Hey, I could cast your runes later, if you want?"

"'Cast my runes'," I mused. "And what exactly do you mean by that?"

"Forecast your future."

"And you can do that?"

"Of course."

"I think on reflection, and without wishing to spurn your offer, I'll leave my destiny un-runed, if you don't mind?"

She laughed.

I pointed through the windscreen. "White Hart Lane."

"What's that?"

"Ah… Now that, I'll have you know, is the home of the mighty Tottenham Hotspur football club."

She nodded towards the stadium. "Do you go to the games?"

"Every home game without fail, and the occasional away match if it's in London."

"Mmm… I knew you liked football, but I didn't know you were obsessive."

"You 'knew'?" I said.

"An interview you did for *Vector* magazine, back in the nineties."

"You have copies going that far back?"

"I've been a member of the BSFA since I was thirteen, and I bought the back numbers that contained anything about you: interviews, reviews, the odd article you wrote."

"Fanaticism indeed. Should I be worried, I ask myself?"

"Do you think I pose a threat?"

I looked her over. "On the whole, no."

She glanced in the rear-view mirror and accelerated.

"Look," I said, "I hope you don't mind my asking, but do you think we're being followed?"

The pink tip of her tongue appeared at the side of her mouth as she thought about it. "I'm not sure. Maybe."

"*I* was joking," I said. "But *you're* not?"

She shook her head. "No, I'm not joking."

"But who…?" I began.

"An ex-boyfriend. He has issues."

I looked at her. "Issues?"

"We met after he emailed to say he loved my posts, and that he was in the music business too. We hooked up. It was good for a while, but he was needy and…"

"And?"

"And it turned out he was using me. I'd just signed the deal with EMI. This was three years ago – "

I stared at her, aghast. "He's been stalking you for *three* years?"

"No, two years."

"Even so… Have you informed the police?"

"No, but they'd be useless. I know they would."

"Are you worried? I mean, is he threatening? Violent?"

"No… No, he's more psychological than that."

"Psychological?" I watched her. She gripped the apex of the wheel and stared straight ahead. I felt suddenly, stupidly, protective. "In what way, Penny?"

"Look," she said, flicking me a glance, "is it okay if we don't talk about it?"

"Yes, of course it is. I'm sorry, I didn't mean to pry."

"I know you didn't. It's just… I really don't know *how* to talk about it, about him, okay? Maybe later, some time, when we're drunk, hmm?"

I smiled. "Of course," I said, and stared ahead at the streaming traffic.

We left London on the M1, and the big blue signboards pronounced, ominously, "The NORTH". I was born in Dorset and have rarely ventured further north than Watford, and when I have, I haven't particularity liked what I've seen. Grim industrial cities, tiny terraced houses, bleak moorland…

Another of my irrational prejudices, as Ursula – from Cheshire – had been fond of pointing out.

At one point, Penny said, "Do you mind if I put some music on?"

"Of course not."

"What do you like?"

I gritted my teeth. "Oh, put on whatever you want."

Oh, Christ, I thought, what the hell have I let myself in for?

"Hokay. Ah … have you heard any of my music?"

"As a matter of fact… Sorry, no."

"Would it seem big-headed of me if I played you some?"

"No, not at all."

She reached out, inserted something into the dashboard – a memory stick or some such – and fiddled with the controls.

"My last album, *Summer Pastorale*… It's a themed album about love, and the land, and haunted England… Here we go."

I girded my loins and gripped the bucket seat. I find the act of listening to music in company excruciatingly embarrassing. And to listen to music when the singer-songwriter is present… My instinct was to jump from the car and run for my life.

Instead, a captive audience, I sat and listened.

Delicate… That was how I'd describe her voice, incredibly soft and breathy, almost inaudible, while her guitar playing was correspondingly gentle and plangent. She sang of mist-shrouded dawns, hazy sunsets, ghosts from the past, mythical figures, unrequited love between fair maidens and tragic beaux…

Her subject was everything I hated: fey romanticism and coy sentimentality, and the cynic in me was repulsed. I had to admit, however, that her music was achingly beautiful, and it moved me.

It would echo in my head for a long time, damn it.

The last dying note faded and we sat in silence for a while as we sped along the motorway.

"That was beautiful," I said at last. "You're very talented, Penny."

"Thank you, Ed," she murmured.

*

Dear Tuppy,

It's been a long time, love. We watch your YouTube posts all the time. Uncle Den bought your first CD round the other night – we didn't know it was out. Lovely. We're so proud of you.

Not much happening at this end. We're doing okay. Den's heart is playing up, but then it always is. Auntie Sue sends her love, and asks when you're coming up.

We miss you, Tuppy. Please get in touch – I'm sure we can sort things out.

Your loving mum,

Dee.

– From a letter sent, c/o EMI Records Ltd, London, to Tuppy Cotton, 2016

*

Rather than stop at a service station, which she told me she hated, she left the motorway. We had coffee and a sandwich in a small town in the Midlands, then continued on our way.

I noticed that she was no longer glancing in the rear-view mirror and mentioned this.

"No, I'm pretty sure he hasn't followed us," she said.

"How often does he?"

"Every so often. He's just there, watching me, in a crowd, staring, or across the street."

"But what does he want?"

She pursed her lips. I thought she was about to tell me, but then shook her head. "I don't know."

"Well, you can forget about him for a while," I went on.

"If he isn't already at the village," she said. "He's often there when I get back from London."

"How often do you come up to Yorkshire?"

"It's the other way around. I live there most of the time, and go down to London on business for a couple of days every month or so. I have a little flat in Camden Town."

I whistled. "I'm in the wrong profession."

She was silent for a time, perhaps wondering how to respond. At last she said, "I give most of my money away, you know? I don't exactly like being rich. I give to charities and good causes."

"Dogs homes?" I said, and wished I hadn't sounded so glib.

"Animal charities. Cancer. Mencap. Greenpeace. Parkinson's. Friends of the Earth. Oxfam. Christian Aid. The Samaritans..." She almost chanted the litany as if to counter my cynicism.

I was cowed. I murmured, "You're a good person, Penny. I'm sorry if I sounded..."

"I felt guilty," she interrupted, "when I signed the deal with EMI and the money started rolling in. More money than I knew what to do with. I bought the manor house, because it was falling down and I fell in love with it, and the flat in London, and the car. After that," she shrugged, "I decided to get rid of ninety per cent of what I earn every month."

I said, "If you don't mind me asking, why are you doing the book if you don't need the money?"

She gripped the apex of the steering wheel. "Why did you start writing, Ed?"

The question wrong-footed me. "Well... It's hard to think that far back."

"Come on!"

"Okay... Because I was inspired by others. Because I had to write, to express myself, to tell *stories*... It's honestly hard to think back and try to work out my motivations. But all of the above. And then I kept on because I had to, and to be honest, I still get an endorphin rush when I write." I smiled. "And I need the dosh."

She shrugged. "I write for the same reason I compose my songs and sing – because I need to. And I, too, am inspired."

She fell silent.

An hour and a half later we left the motorway again, and wended our way along the B roads and winding lanes of Yorkshire.

"But this is beautiful," I said at one point.

"The view from Otley Chevin is one of my favourites."

The land rolled, lush and green, hazed with misty afternoon sunlight; fields divided by dry-stone walls, swathes of dark woodland that followed the undulating contours of the land, snaking rivers and small, honey-coloured villages. We passed through the market town of Skipton and struck north.

"Almost there," she said.

"Apparently there's a good pub not far from your pile," I said.

"How do you know?"

I told her about Guy Lincoln.

"So you checked up on me?"

"I wanted to know what his experience of working with you was like."

"And what did he say?"

"It was a breeze," I said. "He said you were a nice kid."

"Patronising git."

"What did you make of Guy?" I asked.

"Sad case. He seemed unstable, and he drank like a fish. He kept pretty much to himself and almost lived in the pub."

"That sounds like Guy. I expect I'll spend a few evenings there, too. Do you know what it serves?"

"The Knotted Oak?" She shrugged. "I don't know. I never go in. I don't like the place."

I glanced at her. "Why's that?"

She looked uncomfortable. "I don't like the landlord, okay?"

I nodded and let the matter drop.

Presently, we climbed a winding lane and came to the crest of the hill. Penny eased the car to a halt and wound down her window. A warm breeze eddied in, freighted with country smells

– manure and something more fragrant and floral – along with birdsong.

Penny sighed. "I just love this view."

The hillside shelved away to a vale, rising miles away to a moorland escarpment. A tiny village sat amid a network of dry-stone walls: a village green, perhaps fifty stone-built houses, a church standing in an old graveyard, and a public house.

She pointed to a patch of woodland a mile to the east of the village. Nestled amid the trees was a stately house with mullioned windows and multiple chimneys; its aged stonework was almost as green as the surrounding land. Indeed, it seemed one with the countryside in a way I find hard to describe: solid, embedded, permanent.

"Esher Manor," she said. "My house."

She released the handbrake and we rolled down the hill towards the village, but halfway down, I saw a sign and cried out, "Stop!"

"Ed?" she said, braking.

I sat very still and stared at the timber sign that welcomed the traveller to Allenby Wold.

I pointed, and repeated the name.

"My word," I said. "What a coincidence! Do you know something, a writer I read, many years ago – I've got all his books – George Lattimer. He lived here – lives here, as a matter of fact!"

"George? Yes, he does. In fact," she went on, grinning at me, "he owned the manor house. I bought it from him four years ago, when he decided he couldn't look after the place."

"Good God, what a small world. And you say he still lives in the village?"

"He bought a small cottage near the church."

"I'd love to meet him," I said. "If I'd known, I'd have brought some of his books along." I smiled: I sounded like a teenage fan.

Penny frowned. "Well… George had to go into a nursing home a few weeks ago, over in Scarborough. He isn't well. I don't know when he'll be back."

"That's disappointing. I hope he'll…" I hesitated. "How old is he, exactly?"

"In his late nineties, I think. Ninety-seven or -eight."

She set off again and we drove through the village. As we crawled along the narrow main street, I was aware that Penny seemed nervous, glancing left and right at the few cars parked up outside the stone cottages around the green. She seemed relieved when we left the village and motored along the lane towards the manor.

"Your stalker…?" I began.

"Well, his car's nowhere to be seen, so maybe he isn't here."

I nodded, more than a little concerned for her.

At the manor, Penny found a big cardboard box of groceries in the front porch, and explained that she'd rung a Mrs Grieves to get a few things in for her return. She produced a big key and opened the solid oak door.

"Good God, it's like something from a film," I said as we stepped into the mahogany-panelled hallway with a carved timber staircase rising to a gallery landing high above.

"It was in a bit of a state when I bought it," she said. "It took a couple of years to restore. Come on, I'll show you to your room, and then I'll make dinner. Will quiche and salad with fresh bread be okay?"

"Wonderful."

"And I really must get some work done afterwards. I'm behind with some YouTube stuff. Will you be able to entertain yourself?"

"I should think so," I assured her. "I might even give the Knotted Oak the benefit of my custom."

We ate in what Penny called the Great Hall, a vast room with huge timber rafters and a stone fireplace bigger than my kitchen in Hackney. During the meal, she announced that she had a surprise in store for me tomorrow. I wanted to know more, but she repeated that it was a *surprise*, excused herself, and went to work.

I repaired to my room to let the meal digest before I went to the pub. I unpacked my ancient, bulky laptop, read through the first couple of chapters of Penny's MS, and after an hour, made my way along the creaking landing. As I went, I heard her voice from behind a tiny, blackened timber door. She was singing. I paused to listen, unaccountably moved by the sound.

She came to the end of the song and I moved off.

As I was descending the staircase, I heard a door open and Penny call, "Ed?"

"Here." I turned.

She appeared above me on the landing, and a shaft of late sunlight slanted in through a stained-glass window and illuminated her, giving the girl the glowing, ethereal quality of an angel. I found my throat constricted.

"I thought I heard you. These floorboards... Look, you'll find a key hanging on the wall beside the front door. Will you take it with you, and make sure you lock the door when you leave?"

"Look, if you'd feel safer, I can stay here." But she was having none of it. "I'll be fine. I'm here alone all the rest of the time, aren't I? Off you go an enjoy a pint."

"Just as long as you're sure...?"

"Shoo!" she laughed.

I locked the great front door behind me and made my way to the Knotted Oak.

*

The highlight of the anthology is George Lattimer's poignant "The Visitor", in which strange beings are assisted by a human when they venture to Earth: they bestow on him a remarkable gift as a measure of their gratitude. It's a favourite trope that Lattimer has used often in his SF – inter-species cooperation (most famously in his novel The Green Portal*) – and he employs it here to great effect. In its compassion and humanity, Lattimer's tale is reminiscent of Clifford D. Simak's classic "A Death in the House".*

– From J. Cawthorn's review, in *New Worlds* 167, October 1966, of *Transit to Tomorrow* edited by John Carnell, Corgi Books

*

I'd fully prepared myself to be disappointed with the hostelry. I was expecting some run-down country pub patronised by a gallery of inbred yokels, one with all the atmosphere and charm of a public urinal serving some third-rate local brew at four pounds a pint. Guy Lincoln might have been happy enough with the place, but then he's a bipolar alcoholic with low expectations.

My first impressions, of the exterior at least, were favourable: it was an old stone building situated next to the church with well-kept flower baskets hanging along its frontage and a chalked sign beside the door reading: "EIGHT GUEST ALES". Encouraged, I made my way to the main bar: a low-beamed room with an inglenook and padded settles around the walls. There was no sign of the bane of modern public houses: jukeboxes or pool tables. Perhaps a dozen locals occupied the bar – none of them exhibiting any sign of congenital imbecility – and one or two of them even nodded in greeting as I approached the bar.

I was spoilt for choice: Timothy Taylor's Landlord Dark, Theakston's Old Peculier, and a range of Samuel Smith's ales.

I ordered a pint of Landlord Dark, a dark beer thickened and flavoured with caramel, and considered the prospect ahead: three or four weeks working on the book in the afternoons, and evenings propping up the bar at the Knotted Oak. Did life get any better?

I took an appreciative mouthful and regarded my fellow drinkers. As a southerner, and a city dweller, I admit to having preconceived notions of what constitutes northern country folk: I might not have expected dour taciturn men in flat caps, with conversation limited to ferrets and whippets, but I did expect a certain insularity and standoffishness.

But my metropolitan prejudices were dispelled, and soon I was chatting away to a group of villagers about the farce of Brexit, the lunacy of Donald J. Trump, and Scottish independence, among other topical issues.

They were intelligent, informed and humorous, and within an hour, I felt wholly at home.

"I run a second-hand bookshop in Otley," a grizzled sixty-year-old called Tony with a lived-in face and broken nose told me proudly, "and I won a competition for the rudest bookshop proprietor in Yorkshire last year."

"And this year he's going for the title of the rudest in all England," Steve, his corpulent and sandalled friend, put in.

"My job would be great without the sodding customers," Tony went on. "Buggers come in, look at the books, then buy them cheaper on Amazon."

"Don't you sell online?" I asked.

His partner Pru, a strapping, handsome woman in her forties, explained, "Tony has a particular antagonism towards computers and all things technical."

I shook Tony's hand. "You're not alone. I work on a damned PC all day and despise the things."

One of the group, Nigel – a genial red-faced cove in his fifties, who I later learned was a solicitor – asked what my line was, and I told them.

"Bloody hell," Tony said, "the place attracts 'em like a magnet."

Steve asked, "What was the name of that odd chap who practically camped here a few years back?"

"Guy," Pru said. "Sad case. I picked up one of his books, soon after meeting him. Wish I hadn't. I don't like horror at the best of times, but I bridle at graphic descriptions of women having their entrails sucked through their anuses by industrial vacuums."

I winced. "That sounds like Guy," I said. "He'd write anything for filthy lucre. Much like all of us poor hacks."

"You know him?" Pru regarded me as if I'd admitted to a passing acquaintance with Adolf Hitler.

"A business contact," I said. "He's okay."

Something in Pru's expression told me that she'd made the connection between Guy and myself, and our business in the village, and was going to pursue it when Nigel said, "And then there's old George… He wrote sci-fi back in the day, I think."

"George Lattimer," I said. "Now I've never met him, but I grew up on his *science fiction*."

"Any good?" Tony asked.

"A reliable entertainer, and prolific. Yes, some of his better books are excellent adventures." I finished my pint and insisted on buying the next round.

"I'd like to meet Lattimer," I went on. "I understand he still lives in the village?"

"He does," Steve said, "but he's a bit of a recluse these days. We rarely see him around, and he never comes in here."

"Well, he is in his late nineties," Tony said.

"He's never been the same since the explosion," Pru said.

Tony interrupted, "If it was an explosion, Pru…"

I looked around the group. "Explosion?"

"Five years back, would it be, just before he sold the place?" Nigel said. "In the early hours of one Sunday morning. We all heard it."

"All the village heard it," Pru said. "Woke everyone."

"What happened?" I asked.

Tony shook his greying mane and rubbed his broken nose. "No one really knows."

"Let's face it," Steve said, "we don't really know that it came from the manor."

"Well, it sounded as if it came from that direction," Nigel said.

"But surely the police were called in?" I said.

"A local constable went up to the manor on the Monday morning," Pru said, "and had a word with George."

I looked at her. "What did the bobby say?"

She shook her head. "He found nothing at all to suggest there'd been any kind of explosion."

Tony nudged her. "But tell Ed about what Sam Whitaker saw."

"Sam? He's sozzled half the time. You don't take anything he says seriously."

"Still…"

She sighed. "Sam's our local poacher," she explained. "If you ever fancy a nice bit of knocked-off game – a pheasant, or a rabbit or two – Sam's your man. Anyway, he got into the grounds of the manor one day a few weeks after the explosion, setting traps for hares, when he saw one of the outbuildings behind the house. Or rather, he saw what was left of it. Reduced to rubble, he said."

"Why hadn't the local bobby spotted that?" I asked.

Pru smiled. "Old Tom isn't the brightest of the bunch."

"So the explosion, the destroyed building…?" I began.

Nigel shrugged. "Simple explanation, there was a gas boiler or something in there and it went up. But you know how much some folk like conspiracy theories."

"Such as?" I was intrigued.

Tony said, "Some thought George had graduated from writing sci-fi to creating some kind of device up at the manor, like a mad inventor, and it all went wrong. Rubbish, of course. Nigel's right."

"But didn't anyone quiz Lattimer?" I asked.

Pru shook her head and sipped her gin and tonic. "It was soon after this that George fell ill. He shut himself away and rarely came in here. Before then, he came in every Saturday night for a meal and a couple of pints, as regular as clockwork."

"He became a recluse, all right," Nigel agreed, "but I don't think the two are in any way connected. He was simply knocking on, and in my opinion, he was finding it hard to make ends meet. Which is why he finally sold the pile a few years back."

Pru looked at me over her drink. "Is that why you're here? That girl up at the manor wants you to help her with her latest book?"

59

"That's right," I said, taking a mouthful of ale. "I'm here for the next three weeks or so." I raised my drink. "And I'm glad I've found this place," I added.

Nigel eyed me. "So what do you make of Tuppy Cotton, our most recent reclusive celebrity?"

"She's a lovely kid," I said, sounding like an old man even to my own ears. "I can't say I'm into that kind of music, but she has talent." I hesitated. "But you say she's reclusive?"

"She is now," Steve explained, "ever since she was barred from this place."

I lowered my pint and stared at him. "She was *barred* from here?"

Pru nodded. "After she tried to glass her boyfriend. This was a couple of years ago."

I stared at her. "*Glass her boyfriend...?*"

"It wasn't the first time they'd come to blows," Tony said.

Nigel grunted a laugh. "Regular source of entertainment, Tuppy and Timothy. They came in here three or four times a week, and you could be assured that they'd end up arguing once or twice. I lost count of the times Vic had to manhandle the pair out into the lane."

"And then it got violent," Pru added. "One Friday night, we were all in here when Tuppy and Timothy – they were sitting at that table," she pointed across the room to a brass-topped table by the hearth, "when Tuppy broke her glass and lunged at him. Missed him by *this much*, and old Reg managed to wrestle her to the ground. Vic had no option but to bar the both of them."

"Who's this Timothy?" I asked.

Tony shrugged. "Some chap from Leeds, apparently. Never had much to say for himself. Smart, well-dressed. I've seen him about the village a few times since."

I wondered if Timothy was Penny's stalker.

Steve stared into his pint. "Thing is, they were okay before the accident," he said. "I reckon he blamed her for his injuries, and that's what soured their relationship?"

"Accident?" I said.

"One winter's night, a bit over a couple of years back," Nigel said. "They'd been in here for a late session on the way back from Leeds. She should have left her car here and walked – it's only a mile or so to the manor. But she drove ... even through the lane was treacherous with ice. She took the corner near the manor too fast, left the road and ploughed up the verge and into a tree. The car was a write-off, and they were both badly injured. The lad lost his left hand. Almost bled to death. Fortunately, someone saw the accident, gave first aid and called an ambulance."

Steve said, "And that's when the rot set in, I reckon. They were never the same after that. Always bickering, then fighting."

"Ending in the attempted glassing," Pru said.

"That's terrible," I said inadequately. "She seems such a sweet girl."

Talk turned to other matters; Tony complained about a particularly obnoxious customer he'd had in his shop that day, and Steve said that such people were drawn to the place by Tony's reputation. Pru – who was a purser on a Caribbean cruise ship – had evidently returned home from Antigua just two days ago. "People say I'm a lucky so-and-so. But do you know something? When I'm out there, on the ship, all I think about is getting back to the Knotted Oak."

I drank to that.

I was draining my fifth pint when I noticed that it was after midnight.

"Good God, does this place never close?"

"You're in the country, now, Ed. Vic usually calls time around two. How about one for the road?"

"Why not indeed?" I agreed.

It was after one-thirty when I finally gave in and insisted that I must be getting back. I said my drunken goodbyes to my new-found friends, staggered from the pub, and headed east towards the manor.

It was a balmy night beneath the velvet heavens. As I wove my way along the lane, I marvelled at how bright the stars were, with the chiffon spread of the Milky Way arcing overhead. I find that drunkenness concentrates the mind wonderfully on the simple things of life, and all I could think about was the happy accident of coming upon such a pleasant pub and friendly people, and the fact that very soon I would be almost thirty grand richer.

I have no idea how long it was before I realised I was being followed, or quite how it was that I *knew*. Almost subliminally aware that I was not alone, that there was someone in the lane behind me, I staggered towards a dry-stone wall and answered a call of nature. This took some time, owing to the quantities I'd downed that evening. I was sighing with relief when movement made me look to my left, back along the lane.

I thought I saw the inky shadow of a human form step off the lane and merge with an overhanging bush. Perhaps I should have felt alarm at this, but all I thought was that the figure was that of another homeward-bound drinker. I finished what I was doing, zipped up, and continued on my way.

Only when I came to the turning in the lane that led up the long driveway towards the manor house did I stop, swaying, and peer back into the darkness. I saw no figure, but I did make out something – the tell-tale glow of a cigarette as it was lifted towards an invisible face.

I continued on my way to the manor, and after a minute or two spent playing silly buggers with the key and the elusive keyhole, let myself into the premises and locked the door behind me.

SEVEN

I awoke at eight with a surprisingly clear head, made my way downstairs, and found a note on the kitchen table:

I don't do breakfast. See you in the library at eight-thirty. (It's the first door on the right in the west wing.) – P.

I found a tin of ground Arabica, milk and bread, and made myself my customary breakfast of strong coffee and two slices of toast. There was even a jar of yeast extract in the fridge. I spread it thickly on my toast and put the jar in a cupboard, with a mental note to myself to tell Penny that yeast extract should in no circumstances ever be kept in the fridge. It was one of Sula's bad habits that had driven me to distraction.

I returned to my bedroom for my laptop and notes, and wandered along to the west wing.

The library was a long, low room with sunlit French windows at the far end, bookshelves on either side, and a comfortable sofa before a marble mantelpiece.

Penny was curled on the sofa, barefoot, reading a manuscript and cuddling her white rabbit, Ralph. She looked up and gave a dazzling smile. "Morning, Ed. Didn't get too drunk last night?"

"Comfortably merry," I said, smiling at the tiny pixie of a girl who, according to Tony last night, had tried to glass her boyfriend and earned an expulsion from the Knotted Oak.

"I must say, the locals are a friendly bunch."

She returned to her reading, absently stroking Ralph's fluffy pelt. "Are they?"

"I got in with a bookshop owner, Tony, and his partner Pru, and Nigel and Steve. Know them?"

She shook her head. "Can't say I do."

I persevered. "Did you go to the Oak often?"

"A few times, when I first came here."

"Did you go there with your ex, Timothy?"

She looked up, fixing me with her big green eyes. "Has someone been telling you about...?" She trailed off.

"I supposed it had to come out, seeing that I'll be staying here for a while – that you were barred for attacking your boyfriend."

She set her lips in a thin, determined line that reminded me of a reprimanded schoolgirl. "I'm not proud of what I did, Ed. But... Look, he provoked me, okay?"

"I'm not censuring you at all, Penny. The bastard probably deserved everything coming to him." I hesitated. "What did he do?"

She shook her head. "I really don't want to talk about it, if that's okay?"

I smiled. "Fine. No problem. Sorry I mentioned it." I hefted my old laptop. "Right, shall we get to work?"

She watched me with some amusement as I arranged my workplace.

I pride myself on my writing routine: I usually put in two shifts of three hours a day, morning and afternoon, and in that time, produce around four thousand words. In my study, I sit on a sofa, with the keyboard of my PC on my lap. Sula said that this was responsible for my chronic backache, and showed no sympathy when I complained.

I'd brought a separate keyboard and a mouse with me, and pulled a coffee table up before the sofa and set up my laptop.

"What on earth are you doing?" Penny asked.

"This is how I work," I told her. "I can't use the laptop's keyboard – ridiculous things, the mouse too. This set up is far better, with the keyboard on my lap. Now," I said, easing myself back into the soft cushions next to her, "shall we go through the first chapter, and I'll tell you what I intend to do with it?"

"Hokay… I had a few ideas, too," she said.

I outlined the chapter, describing the action, the characters and their motivations, and suggested certain changes.

Penny thought my ideas great, and was not at all precious about her original creation.

"Now, I like the opening. I think it works really well. You set the scene and paint the picture wonderfully, but I'd like to make a few cuts. I'll show you…"

For the next five minutes I went through the first few pages, showing her what I intended to cut and change.

"What do you think?" I said at last.

Lips pursed, she nodded. "I see. Yes, it's much better."

"I don't intend to go through all the MS with you. This will give you the picture. You okay with that?"

"That's fine, great."

"Now, as for the expansions…"

For the next hour or so I explained how I intended to fill out the story, and Penny chipped in with her own ideas, which made sense and which I could easily accommodate. The time flew, and before I knew it, she looked up with an exclamation of surprise, indicated the grandfather clock, and suggested lunch.

"I don't usually bother with lunch," I said. "But I'll have another strong coffee, then start work."

"I'll fix that, Ed, and leave you to it." She jumped from the sofa. "Oh, remember – the surprise?"

"I'd forgotten about that," I said.

"How about I show you later," she said, "around five? I'll be in my room, okay?"

"Very well. I'm intrigued."

I got to work.

*

From a review by A Customer, Amazon US online: *Ed Bentelys book* Transmission Error *was so boring. Whos bothered about a dull love affair between a Brit cop and an African journalist. I wanted action, and I didnt get it. Dosnt even deserve one star. Meh.*

Comment from E Bentley (later removed): *Thank you for that, you fucking illiterate cretin*

*

I looked up some time later, and was surprised to find that almost three hours had elapsed. I did a word count and found that I'd expanded Penny's initial thousand words to a little over three, and I was happy with what I'd written.

I saved the file to a memory stick and closed down my laptop. I rose, yawning, and strolled over to the French windows. It was not yet four o'clock, an hour before I was due to meet Penny. I felt wonderful, basking in the glow of creation that lasts for an hour or so after every shift, but soon fades. The next day, I have to power up my PC and write again, like a drug addict needing his fix.

Sunlight fell on a well-tended back garden, and as I stared across the lawn to a series of outbuildings a hundred yards away, I recalled the conversation last night about the explosion at the manor.

I let myself out through the French windows, and strolled across the lawn.

The outbuildings stood behind a box hedge: a row of stables and a cavernous barn. These were vacant now, but for the accumulated rubbish of years: there was a stack of old kitchen units in one stall, and a jackstraw array of gardening tools, forks, rakes and hoes littered one corner of the barn. I moved along the front of the buildings, unable to spot where an explosion might have occurred.

Then I turned the corner and saw, across a cobbled yard, the tumbledown remains of a building set apart from the others. In the years since its destruction, nature had taken its course; ivy and weeds had grown in amongst the stones, softening their lines and giving the ruins the fake appearance of antiquity. Stepping carefully over the stones, I stood in what would have been the centre of the building, amid the debris of fallen beams and roof tiles.

Something had certainly happened here five years ago. I searched the debris for any sign of electrical equipment or fragments of machinery, anything that might account for the destruction, but found nothing.

I was contemplating returning to the house when I saw Penny. She was sitting on a bench in a formal garden beside the lawn, intent on her phone and oblivious of my presence.

I stepped from the ruins and approached the garden. She looked up, smiling. "Hi, Ed."

I nodded at the phone. "Are you never without that thing?"

"Well, I don't take it in the shower with me, but the rest of the time…"

I sat down beside her and stretched out my legs. "What did you do before you had a phone?"

She turned on the seat and squinted at me. "I've always had one. At least, since I was about thirteen."

"So you can't imagine life without it?"

"No, I can't. I find it hard to believe that you can live without one."

"You pity me?"

She considered the question. "I ... I think you're *missing* something."

I tried not to smile. "What, exactly?"

"Communication, human contact."

"But I don't need superficial human contact to affirm my existence. If I require contact – connection with what it is to be human – then I go to the pub or read Thoreau."

She smiled and looked away quickly, hiding a smile.

"You think I'm a miserable old fart, don't you?" I said. "A curmudgeon who eschews humanity?"

"No, I just think you're just set in your ways, and ... and perhaps frightened of what you don't understand."

I laughed. "Hmm... Maybe, Miss Cotton." I stretched and stared across the garden.

Penny slipped her phone into the pocket of her denim jacket and smiled at me, shielding her eyes against the late afternoon sunlight.

"I wonder if your parents knew what they were doing when they gave you your first phone?"

"Of course they did. And it wasn't out of kindness, you know?"

I looked at her, wondering at the bitterness in her tone. "No?"

"They wanted me out of the way. They didn't want to be bothered with me, and what better way of getting rid of me than giving me a phone? They knew I'd spend all my time on it, which suited them fine. Not that I understood that at the time."

"Are you still in contact?"

"I haven't seen them for years," she said, staring across at the ruins. "That's fine. I left home when I was sixteen, as soon as I could."

"Do you have brothers or sisters?"

"I was an only child. A mistake. My father told me as much. My mother tried to love me, but couldn't really bring herself to, and my father didn't even try. They both resented me for…"

"For?"

She frowned. "For existing, I suppose. For stopping them from doing things… But they were lazy people who would never have amounted to much anyway, and they used my existence as a reason to excuse the hopelessness of their lives. My mother painted, badly, and my father wanted to be a musician, but he didn't apply himself, didn't work at it."

"Are they aware of your success?"

She shrugged. "I've really no idea, and to be honest I don't care." She hesitated. "And don't think that I get a kick from succeeding where they failed, and thinking about how envious they might be. I'm not that shallow."

I shook my head. "I know you're not, Penny."

She reached out her small hand and took mine, squeezing. "Thanks."

She asked me how the novel was coming along, and we talked for a while about the book and how I saw it progressing.

Then she said, "I saw you in the ruins. Your friends at the Oak told you what happened, right?"

"Well, they mentioned an explosion. They didn't know what happened, as such. Do you?"

"No one does."

"Not even George Lattimer?"

"He's … confused about it."

I looked at her. "Confused? It happened in the grounds of his house, just five years ago."

She hesitated. "George is ill. He's had Parkinson's for a long time. That's why he's away at the moment, receiving treatment. He has his good days, but much of the time he's confused, muddled."

69

"Oh…" I said. "Selfishly, I was hoping we could meet, chat about his work."

"Maybe when he gets back," she said. "As I said, he has his good days. And the odd thing is that he can often recall what happened many years ago, but not what happened last week."

"And he can't remember anything about the explosion?"

"I asked him about the ruin while I was buying the manor – I'd heard about it at the pub. But George just looked distant and shook his head. It's sometimes hard to work out what he's heard and understood."

"Someone at the pub – I can't remember who – thought that George's ill health began around the time of the explosion, and that he became reclusive afterwards."

"If his health did begin to deteriorate around then," Penny said, "then I'm sure it was coincidence, don't you?"

I smiled. "More than likely," I agreed.

Then I recalled what Penny had promised me that morning.

"Now," I said, "what about that surprise you mentioned?"

She grinned at me. "Back in the house," she said. "Follow me."

*

My favourite scenario in SF is when aliens come to Earth.
– George Lattimer, interviewed in *New Worlds* 120, July 1962

*

We entered through the French windows, left the library and made our way along to the east wing.

"The house is an ongoing project, Ed. Most of the west wing is refurbished, but there's a lot more to do here. As you can see."

The corridor along which we were walking had seen better days. The wallpaper was peeling in great damp scrolls, the carpet was threadbare, and in many places, the plasterwork of the ceiling had crumbled away. An aroma of damp and mildew pervaded the place.

Penny paused before a big oak door. "Close your eyes, Ed."

I laughed. "Whatever are you showing me?"

"You'll see. Close them."

I did so. I heard the door handle turn, and Penny took my hand and drew me into the room.

"Now open them," she commanded.

"Good God..." I said, staring around at the sunlit room.

"George Lattimer's study," she said, "where he worked on his books for over sixty years."

I have a fascination with writers' workplaces: their studies, libraries, dens all beguile me – and the more books in them, the better. George Lattimer's study was a cornucopia.

The room was long and low, and equipped with built-in mahogany bookcases. These spanned three walls, each one filled with books. The furnishings were old-fashioned and dark: a desk with a portable typewriter, a settee pulled up before an empty hearth, a sonorously ticking grandfather clock.

I said, "But – this is amazing, Penny! How come...?"

She came to my side and stared around the room. "When George showed me around the place, he said that the one regret he would have in selling the manor was that he'd have to get rid of much of his collection. His new place in the village was tiny, with no room for his books. He'd be able to keep his own titles, but not many more..." She shrugged. "I felt sorry for him, and had an idea. I was moving in here by myself. The place was vast, and I wouldn't need all of it. So I said that, if he liked, he could keep his study on here, come back whenever he wanted."

"And he agreed, obviously."

"It was rather touching. He cried. I had to pretend to be absorbed in some of his books while he dried his tears. Anyway, he took me up on my offer, and in the early days after I moved in, he'd take a taxi from the village and we'd have tea in here. Then I'd leave him to read for a while before he returned home. More recently, he hasn't been able to visit as much..."

I crossed the room to a bookcase against the wall beside the desk; it was ranked with perhaps a hundred books, most of them paperbacks with a few hardbacks in amongst: all bore the name of George Lattimer on their spines.

The first twenty or so, on the top shelf, were Ace Doubles. I pulled one or two down, carefully leafing through their pages, reading a line or two and admiring the cover graphics.

I smiled at *Vengeance from Vega* by George Lattimer, with a Jack Gaughan cover depicting a needle-shaped spaceship standing tall on a rocky alien world. The strapline ran: *They came in search of treasure, but terror was their only reward.* On the flip-side of the paperback was an early novel by Philip K. Dick.

"They're truly beautiful," I said, passing the book to Penny.

She smiled at the artefact of a bygone publishing era.

"I still collect these," I told her. "I first read them when I was living in Australia, as a teenager. They did something to me, lodged in here…" I smiled. "They still do something to me. It's almost as if…"

She was looking up at me. "Go on."

"I don't know… It might sound daft, but they filled me with … with *hope*; yes, that's the right word. They came to represent a reality much more hopeful, and I admit, far simpler, than that which surrounded me. I was sixteen and lonely and far from home, and I was seeking something other than the everyday, the mundane. Ace Doubles gave me that something – quite apart from entertaining me with fantastic adventures. They gave me hope for the future … and not only the stories themselves, but the fact that someone wrote them, that there were men and women working away at telling their strange stories of the future… I knew, within days of reading my first Robert Silverberg, that I wanted to do nothing with my life other than write, and write science fiction."

"And you've done it, Ed. You've created books which, no doubt, give hope to youngsters like yourself."

"Hard though that is to imagine," I said, "wearied by cynicism over the years." I shook my head. "I'd very much like to meet George Lattimer, just so that that boy in Melbourne all those years ago can say thank you, at last."

"That would be wonderful," she murmured.

Later, we enjoyed a simple dinner of bread and cheese, and salad. Afterwards, Penny suggested that she open a bottle of wine, and long into the evening, we sat in Lattimer's study and talked about life, the world, and the universe.

EIGHT

Over the course of the next week or so, we fell into an easy routine. We'd meet after breakfast to discuss the next chapter – although increasingly Penny was happy to accept whatever I suggested – and I would get on with it for the rest of the day, producing three or four thousand words. At five o'clock, I'd stop work and meet Penny for a stroll around the grounds of the manor, and then we'd have a leisurely dinner followed by a bottle of wine and conversation.

The weather was glorious, long hot days stretching into balmy evenings. Sometimes we'd sit outside the French windows at the back of the house and watch the sun go down.

On one such evening, ensconced in an armchair I'd pulled from the library, and soporific from the effects of a strong Chilean merlot, a comfortable silence came between us. I simply looked at Penny stretched out on a sun lounger, her wine glass balanced on the strip of bare belly showing between the bottom of her T-shirt and the top of her denim shorts.

At one point, Penny said, "Have you noticed, Ed?"

I squinted at her. "Noticed what?"

"That I've been good."

"Good?"

"I don't have my phone with me when I'm with you…"

I felt a twinge of guilt. "Good girl," I said.

Minutes elapsed. We drank.

A little while later, Penny said, "Do you mind if I ask you a personal question?"

"We've known each other long enough not … not to be phased by enquiries into our intimate lives." I was, I think, a little drunk.

She closed one eye and peered at me. "Does … does that mean, yes, or no…?" She was, quite definitely, a little squiffy.

"It means I don't mind in the slightest."

"Good." She fell silent.

Across the lawn, a rabbit bobbed, and the sun had entangled itself in the upper branches of elm tree. A late bee, homeward bound, meandered drowsily from the herbaceous border.

"Well, Penny, ask away."

"No… It's really too personal."

I took a mouthful of merlot. "Let me guess," I said. "It's about Sula, hmm? Our relationship? You want to know why she left me."

"You've told me that already."

"I have?"

"Three nights ago, in there." She thumbed over her shoulder towards the library.

"I don't remember that. And what did I say?"

"You said … you said that … that you were a sad, lazy, boring old git who deserved to be dumped."

"I did? I said that? Well, well… I must have been drunk to have spoken such truth. *In vino veritas*, as they say."

"But I don't think so," she said.

I peered at her. "You don't think I was telling the truth?"

"No, I know you were telling the truth. But I don't think that you're a sad, lazy, boring old git."

"Why, thank you, Penny Cotton."

"Well, you're maybe a bit lazy, and old, but ... but you're not boring, or sad. Least, I don't think so."

"It warms my heart to hear such an affirming accolade, my child."

"You're welcome," she said, saluting me with an almost empty glass.

I reached for the bottle and poured more wine. Then I slumped back, exhausted from the exertion.

"Ed ... were you upset when your wife left you?"

"Haven't I told you whether or not I was?"

"Can't recall. Don't think so."

"Well... Let me think. Was I upset? Upset? *Up-set*. A strange word. I don't think upset adequately describes my reaction at the time. I felt an odd mixture of emotions, in no particular order..." I held up my left hand and stuck out a finger, one after the other, to denote each adjective. "Surprise. Regret. Anger. Acceptance. Jealousy. I've run out of fingers. "Relief..."

"Relief?" She sounded surprise.

"Relief," I repeated. "But is that the right word? From time to time, I do feel an odd sense of ... liberation. A certain freedom from routine and requirements that had become ingrained. I can do whatever the hell I wish, dress as slovenly as I want, get as pissed as I like... However, the sense of freedom is sometimes overtaken by any one of the aforesaid emotions. Do I make myself plain, my girl?"

"I ... I think so. Nothing is ever simple and straightforward. Life is complex. Emotions are complex, and our ... our reactions to experience are never ... never just black or white, but a ... a complex interplay of chiaroscuro."

"Jesus Christ!" I said. "Did you really say chi-chi ... whatever ... after one and a half bottles of plonk?"

"I rather think I did."

"Brilliant!"

"Do you hate Ursula for walking out on you?" she asked.

I waved. "No. No… We all feel trapped in our lives, at times. I suppose … I suppose it's natural to rail against circumstance and lash out at those close to us, to try to hurt them."

I took another mouthful of wine and reached for the bottle, only to find that it was empty.

Like the little champion she was, Penny Cotton tottered to her lovely bare feet and weaved her way into the house. She emerged a long time later bearing another bottle of red.

"Sorry. Had to pop along to the loo. It's miles away."

It took me a long time to unscrew the lid. Thank Christ it wasn't a cork…

I did the honours.

We sat back.

I closed my eyes. The night was still warm. Somewhere far off, birds sang.

"I remember!" Penny cried out, startling me.

I opened my eyes. The twilight was the hue of rosé wine.

"You remember what?"

"What I was going to ask you."

"I thought you'd already asked me. About how I felt when Sula left me?"

"No, no… That wasn't the question. It was … it was this: would you have liked to have had a daughter?"

She hiccupped and blinked at me as I stared at her.

"What an odd question," I murmured.

"Is it? But would you? Did you want a daughter? Did Ursula?"

I pointed at her. "Why do you state specifically a 'daughter'? Why not a son?"

She shrugged. "Dunno." She stared at me. "Well?"

I thought back over the years, all twenty-five of them, and the alcohol dulled the pain.

A year after I met Sula, a year after I fell head over heels in love with her – and she with me, presumably – she announced she was pregnant. I was overjoyed. We married quickly, and I looked forward to the unexpected but wholly welcome prospect of becoming a father –

– of a girl, the scans decreed.

To cut a long story very short – and I don't like writing about it, even now – Sula went into labour and we took a taxi to hospital, and twelve hours later, our daughter (we'd agreed to name her Ella) was born, and was diagnosed with a heart condition soon after. She died in hospital six months later.

Drunkenly, I gave Penny a précis of the above.

"Sula," I finished, "was devastated. She never really recovered."

Penny blinked at me. "Didn't you ... try for another?"

I looked away, pained by her question, and ignored it. "I ... I put it behind me. I tried to forget the plans I'd made, the anticipation. Do you know, I'd looked ahead, seen Ella at ten, at fifteen... At twenty, having lunch with me when I visited her at college..." I fell silent, then said, "Silly, isn't it?"

"No ... not silly at all."

She reached out her small hand towards me. I stared at it as it hung between us. I had never noticed her hands, her fingers, until now, never noticed how perfect they were, and how flawless.

I reached out and took her fingers, kissed them, then held them in silence as the sun went down and twilight descended.

A little later her words stirred me from long-forgotten memories. "Ed?"

I opened one eye. "Mmm?"

"Do you know what I want you to do?"

"What ... what do you want me to do?"

"Ed, would you pick me up and ... and carry me inside, and up to bed, and tuck me in, please?"

I squinted at her. "Are you sure?"

"Absolutely. Tuck me up in bed."

Which is exactly what, despite my drunkenness, I managed to do.

*

Ed Bentley's latest novel shows why he's at the forefront of British SF writers: he tells a well-paced story peopled with characters you come to care about – and the core idea is wholly original. Recommended.

– Peter F. Hamilton, cover blurb for *Destination Ophiuchi* by Ed Bentley, Worley and Greenwood, 2012

*

The following day, after dinner, I asked Penny if she would like to accompany me to the Knotted Oak. Before she could remind me, I held up a hand and said, "I'll have a word with the landlord, slip him a few quid, and he'll unbar you lickety-split."

She pulled a face and said that she was really behind on all her YouTube stuff, and that she had to broadcast her latest composition tonight. "But I'd love to another time."

So I went alone, and, in light of what happened later that evening, perhaps that was just as well.

*

"The essence of contemporary speculative fiction…"

– Bob Shaw, cover quote for Ed Bentley's *Capricorn Days*

*

The Knotted Oak overlooks the village green. A wooden bench stands to the left of its entrance, and a beer garden extends along the side of the premises to a long, lawned area at the rear. It was after eight when I arrived, but still warm, and I bought a pint of Old Peculier and carried it outside. I sat on the bench beneath the pub sign depicting the eponymous oak tree, found a copy of

The Yorkshire Post left by a previous drinker, and leafed through it at my leisure.

There are few pleasures greater than the enjoyment of a good pint on a summer's evening while absorbing the woes of the world through the distancing medium of newsprint. Perhaps my good mood was helped by having logged on that afternoon to find that *Daily Science Fiction* had bought one of my short stories, which would pay for my next curry and a few pints. The novel was also going well: I had almost forty thousand words in the bag and foresaw no hitches along the way.

I was enjoying Penny's company. Truth to tell, I was not looking forward to when I finished the book and my time with her came to an end. I decided that we must keep in contact; I would take her out for lavish meals when she was in London.

I finished my pint and went inside for another, Smith's extra stout this time.

I returned to the bench and read the sports section of the paper: the Yorkshire cricket team was losing to Surrey, and Leeds United had just signed a new striker.

A few locals were occupying tables outside the pub, mainly couples, and one or two families. I was hoping that Tony, Pru and the others would be along later, and that we could renew our acquaintance from my first visit to the pub.

When I finished reading the paper and laid it aside, I noticed a young man seated at a nearby table. He was watching me, and he nodded and smiled at my glance.

"I hope you don't mind…" he began nervously. "But aren't you Ed Bentley, the SF writer?"

"That depends," I quipped, "on whether you didn't like my last one and want your money back."

He smiled. "Don't worry. I've enjoyed your books. Would you mind if I joined you?"

"Be my guest."

He was a tall, slim, well-groomed fellow in his mid-twenties, with the dark good looks that are helped by five o'clock shadow.

He wore designer jeans and a white shirt, and a gold chain hung around his tanned neck.

"I really enjoyed the *Titan* trilogy," he said, sitting down. It was only later that I noticed he wasn't drinking.

"Ah," I said, "the ground-breaking work, which was destined, in my mind at least, to propel me to SF stardom, and which in fact sold abysmally." I raised my pint. "But I'm delighted you liked the books."

We chatted about the possibility of terraforming Titan – he was well versed on the subject – and I was wondering how he'd recognised me when he mentioned that someone in the pub had said I was staying with Penny Cotton up at the manor.

"That's right," I said. "We're working on a book together." I offered to buy him a pint. For some odd reason, I find it hard to appreciate my beer when my company is abstemious.

He thanked me and said he'd like a half of mild. Lightweight, I thought as I went to the bar.

I returned with his half, and another pint for myself, and resumed my seat.

He raised the glass in thanks, took a sip, then slipped a cigarette between his lips and lit it with a Zippo lighter.

One of the many things that Sula said about me was that, for a writer, I was totally unobservant. By this she meant that I missed things that she noticed. In my defence, I pointed out that I noticed things that were important to me.

And she'd replied, "Exactly my point, Ed. Most things *aren't* important to you."

How did I miss that the young man – who never introduced himself, by the way – had kept his left hand below the level of the table during our conversation?

"How are you getting on with Penny?" he asked.

"Very well. She's a bright kid." I cursed myself for sounding so patronising.

"She is. Beauty and brains."

"You local?" I asked, finishing my previous pint and centring the new one on the beer mat.

"Leeds," he said, and even then, I failed to make the connection.

I gestured to the green, the village in general. "It's a beautiful spot. What are you doing here?"

He was evasive. "Just visiting…"

Around this point, I began to get a little uncomfortable. The conversation was stilted. He seemed nervy, as if he wanted to ask me something, but could not bring himself to do so.

He licked his lips, then rephrased an earlier question. "How … do you find Penny?" he asked.

I lowered my pint. "In what way?"

"I mean … don't you think she's a bit … odd?"

I smiled. "Odd? Well, she's quirky, original, sensitive… What do you mean by *odd*?"

He shook his head and stared down at his pint. "Look … me and her…"

Only then did the penny drop.

I said, "You're Timothy?"

He looked up. "She's mentioned me?"

"Only briefly – "

"We were together for almost a year. I loved her. Christ, how I loved her. She's a special woman, you know?"

I nodded. "I know," I said, and felt an odd, irrational kick of jealousy. "She is."

"I was very happy with her. I thought… Well, I thought I'd found the person who…" he trailed off.

"I know what it's like," I said. "When I was your age…" *Christ,* I thought, *just listen to me – the old man bestowing the largesse of his experience on callow youth.* "And even now, when someone you love walks out…"

He stared at me. "Oh, it wasn't like that."

"She didn't leave you?"

"*I* left *her*," he said.

"Ah…"

But why the hell, I asked myself, should he be stalking her: wasn't the archetype of a stalker someone who'd been jilted and resented the fact?

"Did she tell you what happened?" he asked.

"Happened?"

"That night? The accident?"

"Ah, no. That is, I've heard about it, but…"

He sipped his drink, watching me. He said, "We'd been here. A drink or two… We should have walked back. It's only a mile or so. But it was a cold night. Freezing. She had her car."

He stopped, staring down at his drink. I noticed that he kept his left hand below the level of the table. I thought how terrible it must be for someone so young, and presumably conscious of his good looks, to be maimed as he was.

"Look," I said, "it's all very well blaming Penny for what happened, and perhaps she shouldn't have driven that night…"

He stared at me, slowly shaking his head. "You don't understand," he said, and reached across the table and gripped my wrist.

At that moment, a couple approached along the path to the pub's entrance, then stopped and stared at us. It was Tony and Pru, and Pru was regarding Timothy with an expression of supreme distaste.

"Is he bothering you, Ed?" she asked.

Before I could reply, she nodded to Tony, who hurried into the pub.

"Christ!" Timothy said, releasing his grip on my arm.

Tony emerged from the pub, accompanied by the corpulent landlord, who took one look at the young man and swore.

"I thought I'd told you," he said, standing over Timothy, arms akimbo, "to sling your fucking hook and never come back?" He reached out, and snatched up the young man's barely touched half pint. "Go on, fuck off, and I'm warning you – show your face here again and I'll have the police in, got it?"

Timothy muttered something unintelligible, and with as much dignity as he could muster, rose from the table and strode off.

The landlord nodded to me. "Sorry about that, sir. Pint on the house?"

"Well…" I said, non-plussed.

Pru said, "Joining us inside?"

"Very kind of you," I said, following them into the snug.

"What was all that about?" Tony asked, once we had our pints and were seated around a table by the inglenook.

"Somehow," I said, "he'd found out I was up at the manor, working with Penny."

I told them about the encounter, and my slowness at cottoning on to the young man's identity. "I assumed, from what he was saying about his relationship with Penny, that he resented the end of their relationship. But then he told me that *he'd* left her. So … was it the accident that brought about the split? Did he resent her for his injury?" I shook my head. "But if so, why the hell stalk her?"

Pru glanced at Tony, then shook her head. "He frightens me."

"You don't think," I said, "that Penny's in danger?"

"Well, the way he's obsessively haunting the village…" Tony said. "It makes you wonder what he's up to."

Conversation turned to other matters and the beer flowed. I told them how the novel was coming along, and I gave a long and drunken disquisition on the trials of being a freelance writer in the age of Amazon. Then Tony enumerated the many woes of running a second-hand bookshop, and Pru described the downside of looking after geriatric passengers on Caribbean cruise ships.

It was well after midnight when I decided that I'd had my fill, said goodnight, and wandered away from the Knotted Oak.

A full moon hung above the woodland surrounding the village, silvering the lane and lighting my way. I'd forgotten all about my encounter with the mysterious Timothy; my thoughts were on Penny, and our drunken conversation the previous evening. I recalled carrying her up to her room, Penny almost dozing in my embrace, rolling her into bed and pulling the duvet up around her chin. I recalled sitting by her for a long time, staring at her child's face as she slept. Then I crept from the room so as not to wake her, went downstairs and drank another bottle of wine. I'd still managed to get up at eight and put in a full shift at the laptop.

"Mr Bentley!"

The call startled me. I stood in the lane, swaying, and peered into the darkness ahead.

Then I heard footsteps behind me. The white-shirted figure of Timothy loomed out of the darkness. I blinked at him. "Timothy, Timothy … mysterious Timothy!"

"Mr Bentley, Ed – I need to talk to you."

"Talk away, Timothy. Talk away! My ears are…" I stopped. I didn't know what my ears were. Then I recalled: "Open."

He took a step towards me. I did my best to focus on his serious face.

"It's about Penny," he said.

"Penny…" I echoed. "I understand. In … in your position, I'd feel the same." I gestured at his left arm, which terminated in a white cuff. "I'm sorry. It must be … must be…" I waved in drunken semaphore to indicate how terrible it must be to have only one hand.

"But," I said seriously, "you mustn't hate her, Timothy! Hate … is *not* a good emotion, let me tell you. It's bad, very bad. It corrodes, hate does."

"I don't hate her, Mr Bentley."

That stopped me. "You don't? But then why are you … stalking her?"

He hesitated. "I want to show you something," he went on, taking me by the arm.

"Show me?"

"Along here..."

We walked along the lane like old friends, Timothy's grip steadying my weaving progress.

"A beautiful night," I said. "Timothy, you know, you really shouldn't have gone ... gone and got yourself barred. Silly thing to do, and from the only pub in the village! Reprehensible conduct, sir!"

He pointed. "Here," he said.

A dry-stone wall showed in the moonlight, with the looming shape of an oak tree beyond. I noticed the gap in the wall, and at first, thought it was the opening of a farm gate.

"This is where it happened, Mr Bentley."

In retrospect, I realise that this is where I sobered up a little. "The crash," I murmured.

"The crash," he replied.

"But ... as I said earlier ... you shouldn't hold it against..."

Timothy interrupted me: "It was my fault. You see, it was my suggestion that she drive. It was only a mile, I said, and there would be no traffic."

"But...?"

"So she drove, but the lane was icy, and she took the corner too fast. I remember thinking that the wall was too close... We skidded, hit the wall, went right through it and hit the tree." He pointed at the oak in the darkness.

"I don't know how long I was unconscious for ... but when I came to my senses, I was lying on my back on the grass, over there, and the car was a mangled wreck by the tree."

"And Penny?"

He pointed across the lane towards the gap in the wall. "She'd been thrown from the car ... or had crawled from it."

He paused, staring at where the accident had happened.

"I don't know how long I was lying there. I passed in and out of consciousness, a dull pain throbbing..." He lifted his left arm. "All I wanted to do was crawl across to where Penny was lying and check that she was okay, but I couldn't."

He shook his head. "There was a strange light. I saw a shadowy figure, bending over Penny, doing things to her, stemming the bleeding from her head... The light was odd. The figure approached me, but I passed out again. Later, I learned it was George Lattimer."

"He probably saved your life," I said.

"The next thing I knew, I woke up in hospital. Oh, and the relief when I found out that Penny was alive. But..." He stared at me, bleakly, "but nothing was ever the same between us, after that. I ... I swear I didn't resent her for what happened, for my losing..." He lifted his arm again. "But perhaps I did, on some buried level, and perhaps I let it show without realising it. Things between us got worse. We'd argue over nothing, and for all I could see the rows beginning, there was nothing I could do to prevent them. It was terrible, and it reached the point where I could take no more, so I ended the relationship."

I blinked at him in the darkness. "But ... but why," I said, "are you ... following her now?"

He glazed at me. "Because I realised that I made a mistake, Ed. I love her, and I want her back. And ... and I suppose I resent George Lattimer."

I tried to work out the logic of this. "You resent him for ... for saving your life?" I said.

Timothy gave a humourless laugh. "No. No, of course not. Perhaps I'm wrong, but I resent him for the hold he has over Penny. She'll do anything for him." He rubbed his face with his right hand. "I just want her back, Ed."

I stared at him, feeling a wave of tiredness sweep over me. "Look," I said at last. "Look, Timothy, I'm very drunk. We need to talk. Another day, okay? We'll meet up, you and me, and we'll talk. You're staying in the village?"

He said he was, and gave the name of a guest house near the church.

I reached out and took his shoulder. "We'll talk," I said, with drunken mawkishness.

He nodded, and hesitated, and I thought he was on the verge of saying more, but he just nodded and moved off down the darkened lane.

I watched him go, wondering at the encounter, then made my way back to the manor.

NINE

I decided not to mention my meeting with Timothy when I saw Penny after breakfast. She was happy and bright – she told me that her session had gone well last night – and I outlined how I intended to change the next few chapters. She said that sound great and left me to it.

That evening, as we shared a bottle of wine outside the library after dinner, I said, "Oh, by the way... Last night I met that character, Timothy. He buttonholed me outside the Oak."

"Timothy?" She looked annoyed. "He's here?"

I described our meeting at the pub, and later, in the lane.

"He told me about the accident," I said.

Penny stared at her glass for a time. At last, in a small voice, she said, "He said I was driving too fast, but I swear I wasn't. It was the ice, on the bend. It all happened so quickly. I lost control."

"Is that all you recall?"

"No. I can remember afterwards. I was lying on the grass. I must have been thrown from the car. Lying on my back, staring up at the stars... It's very strange."

I waited, and she went on, "You know those experiences some people have on the verge of death? They're dying, passing down a long tunnel towards a light?" She shrugged. "Well, that happened to me. I was dying. I *know* I was – but the odd thing is that I wasn't afraid. In fact, I felt very calm, peaceful. But…" She shook her head. "But then I had some intimation that it wasn't my time, and I was … *pulled* back. The next thing I knew, I was lying on the icy grass, beside the lane, staring up and the stars … and then I passed out."

She took a small sip of wine. "And then I woke in hospital, and learned that Timothy had survived, but… His hand. And I felt so guilty, Ed."

I gestured, and said inadequately, "He told me he still loves you."

She looked exasperated.

I said, "You don't want to talk about him?"

"Not really."

"You should, you know? It does help, to talk."

She sighed.

"Come on," I said. "You can trust me."

"I know I can," she said. "Look, it was always an uneasy relationship. He was always so … so needy. After the accident, as I said … I felt guilty, and he made it obvious he resented me for what happened that night. That is … he didn't come straight out and accuse me of dangerous driving, but I could see it there in his attitude. And when he finished with me … I think I was relieved – but that made me feel even *more* guilty. Silly, isn't it?"

"Not silly at all, Penny. Quite understandable."

"Anyway, a month or so after the accident, he appeared at the Oak one night and said he'd made a mistake, and would I take him back? I made it obvious it was over. We had a blazing row. That's when … when I attacked him. I don't know what came over me – I just lost it. Anyway, he followed me to London later, and that's when the stalking began."

"You could get a restraining order," I said.

"I don't know… Don't you need proof? And he hasn't actually threatened me."

"That doesn't come into it. He might not be dangerous, but he does seem obsessive. It might be safest if the police were informed."

She nodded, staring down into her wine. "Maybe," she murmured.

We talked of other things for a while, and then Penny looked up, smiling, and said, "Oh, I had a phone call today from the nursing home – George might be discharged pretty soon."

"That's wonderful," I said. "How is he?"

"His medication has been adjusted and he's improving."

"I'm looking forward to meeting him."

"And," she said, "I'm looking into having him stay here. The doctor I spoke to said that he shouldn't really be living alone. He needs nursing care day and night. So…" She shrugged. "I looked into hiring three nurses – he'd have the bedroom just along from his study. It's *en suite*, and there's a room next door that the nurses can use."

"That's very kind of you."

She stared into the distance. "It's the least I can do."

*

I won't beat about the bush, Ed. Your last couple haven't shifted as many units as we'd hoped, so I'll regretfully have to pass on Martian Equatorial.

– From an email to Ed Bentley from Donald Tylesly, commissioning editor at Methuen, 2002

*

Another week passed.

The novel progressed. I wrote another twenty thousand words, and now the end was in sight: one more week and the first draft would be finished.

I alternated between going to the Oak one night, and then staying in with Penny and drinking wine as the sun set. I saw Tony and Pru and the others for a few late sessions, and enjoyed their company; they were decent people, and I would miss them when I returned to London.

One evening, I proposed that Penny and I should go for a walk. At her suggestion, we left the manor by a back lane – avoiding, I noted, the bend where the accident had happened – and wandered up a winding lane to a timber bench high on the hillside. The view was spectacular: Allenby Wold lay at our feet, and the vale stretched away into the sun-hazed distance.

"I've been thinking…" Penny said.

"Mmm?" I should, I thought, have brought a bottle of wine and a couple of glasses.

"Maybe… I don't know, but if you want to, that is…"

I knew what she was coming to. "Go on."

"You'll be doing a second draft, won't you? So … why don't you stay on another week or so. Two weeks? It's been great having you around. We get on well, don't we?

"We certainly do. We're a team, you and me."

"Ace Doubles!" she said. She looked at me, fingering a strand of hair from her brow. "So you'll stay a bit longer?"

"I'd love to, Penny."

She was silent for a time, staring out across the vale. "Every month I go down to London. I told you, I have a little place in Camden. We could always meet up for a meal. And you could come up here for a break whenever you liked."

"That sounds more than wonderful."

I have been at pains during the course of this narrative to underplay the idea that I might have harboured any sexual desire towards Penny Cotton. I would be lying if I denied that I didn't find her attractive: she was young and pretty, and beautiful in spirit. But our relationship went deeper than anything physical. I felt possessive of her, and protective, though these were attributes more paternal than procreative.

We wandered home and shared a late bottle of wine in the library.

Three days later, George Lattimer returned to Esher Manor.

*

Q) Who are your favourite SF writers and why?

A) I have many, but top of the list is Clifford D. Simak for his compassion and humanity. At a time when most American SF writers are writing about aliens as a threat – a thinly veiled reference to the perceived communist threat – Clifford is writing about aliens as neighbours. Another favourite of mine is John Brunner, who tells real SF from a heartfelt liberal standpoint.

– From an interview with George Lattimer conducted for the BSFA magazine *Vector*, July 1960

*

I was tidying up the last paragraph I had written that day when I heard the ambulance crunch up the gravel drive. I moved to the French windows and watched. A medic, accompanied by two nurses, opened the back of the vehicle and assisted George Lattimer from the vehicle.

The old man was over six feet tall and severely thin, with a gaunt face and a full head of gunmetal grey hair. He wore impeccable tweeds and carried himself, I thought, with a certain ancient dignity.

Penny appeared and took his hand. Leaning on a stick, with Penny holding him by his elbow, he limped across the drive towards the house.

At dinner that evening, Penny mentioned she'd told George all about me, and that he said he'd be delighted to meet me later that evening.

"But he tires easily, so don't stay for more than an hour."

I had met many famous people in my time – Nobel-prize-winning writers, film stars and politicians – but it is true to say that I was far more excited at the prospect of meeting George

Lattimer, a hero of my youth, whose books of intrigue and adventure amongst the stars had shaped my life.

*

He was imprisoned for a crime he didn't commit – and then the aliens invaded!
– Strapline for George Lattimer's *The Cassiopeia Enigma*, Ace Books, 1962

*

At seven o'clock, I knocked on the study door, and a rich baritone voice bade me enter.

I had expected George Lattimer, seen at close quarters, to be a shrunken shell of a man, beset with the tremors common to those afflicted with Parkinson's disease. However, as I crossed the room to where he stood before the mantelpiece, I was surprised to see that he appeared in reasonable health. It was remarkable that the tall, gaunt, smiling man before me was just three years shy of his century.

"Edward, so good to meet you at last. I must say how much I enjoyed *The Tithonian Project*. First rate, sir. I think it the very best of your work. I read it again while I was recuperating in that accursed nursing home!" He laughed. "It made the stay bearable."

I murmured my surprise and delight.

He gestured to an armchair, next to which a teapot and cups were set upon a small table.

I was twenty-seven again, almost as tongue-tied as when I'd met Robert Silverberg at a WorldCon in Brighton.

"That's kind of you," I murmured. "I must say, I came across your early Ace Doubles when I was living in Australia in the seventies. I loved your *Time Police* series."

His thin, sallow face creased into a smile. "And I very much enjoyed writing those books, Edward. Oh, it was a fine time to be working, you know, back in the fifties. All those magazines

… and the paperback houses starting up. I can verily say that the world was my oyster."

He asked if I would be so good as to pour the tea, as he found lifting things these days more than a little difficult.

We talked shop for far longer than the hour Penny had stipulated. He regaled me with his meetings with the great and the good of the science fiction universe: how he had shared cocktails in New York with Asimov and Clarke, and partied with Aldiss, Ballard and Harrison at a writers' conference in Spain. He told me of meeting, and arguing with, John W. Campbell Jr at a convention in '65.

"I might have sold numerous tales to *Astounding*, and later *Analog*, but I can't say I saw eye to eye with the man. I mean, Edward, his parochial insistence that when humankind went out among the stars, we would meet and best every alien race there was! Ridiculous, and so blinkered!"

"I could never take his human bias seriously."

"And some of his other views were even nastier. I was at the convention where my old friend John Brunner took Campbell to task over his views on slavery. My word, he made the man look like the fool he was!"

He reminisced, and I hung on his every word.

At one point, he smiled sadly. "Those were the days, Edward, the halcyon days. The world seemed young, with a vibrant future ahead of us – and all the greats of the field were still alive. Sadly now the greats are all dead."

"You're the last of the old guard, Mr Lattimer."

"My friends," he said, "call me George."

A little later, noting the time and recalling Penny's injunction, I said that I really must say goodnight.

"One other thing, my boy," he said, and laid a thin, restraining hand on my arm. "Penny mentioned that you've met Timothy."

"Ah, yes. Yes, I have."

He pursed his lips and nodded. "We need to talk again, you and I." He lowered his voice. "Tomorrow night, Penny is doing one of her broadcasts, so could you possibly sneak a bottle of wine in here at seven, and I'll ... I'll tell you all about *that* business, hmm?"

I said that I'd be more than delighted to do so, and took my leave.

I slept badly that night, going over my conversation with George Lattimer and wondering just what he might have to tell me.

TEN

"How did it go with George last night?" Penny asked me the following morning.

"Very well. He's an amazing chap. Some of the stories he had to tell… It was wonderful to talk to someone who knows so much about the genre. And I was pleased to see that he didn't seem to be as ill as I feared he might be."

"He's up and down," she said. "Yesterday was one of his better days." She hesitated. "Did he mention the accident?"

I answered truthfully. "No, he didn't."

He had mentioned Timothy, let it be said, and alluded to "*that business*", but I don't think I was being deceitful to Penny when I said that he hadn't actually mentioned the accident as such.

"I have to do a broadcast tonight. I've composed another song – it'll be on the next album, and EMI are keen for me to publicise it. I was wondering if you could drop by and see George again?"

"I'd be more than happy to," I said.

*

One of my proudest moments was at a convention in London when Michael Moorcock crossed the room, shook my hand, and thanked me for a story of mine he'd just accepted for New Worlds. *And I'd always thought he considered me old school!*

– George Lattimer, interviewed in *Vision of Tomorrow* 3, 1970

*

At seven that evening, I liberated a bottle of ten-year-old grenache from the cellar and knocked on the study door.

A frail summons greeted me, and I entered the room to find Lattimer seated in an armchair before the empty hearth, a plaid blanket covering his lap. He smiled up at me, but he seemed a little frailer this evening, somehow reduced. His face was as sallow as old parchment, and his right hand shook as he pointed to the bottle I carried.

"I see you've brought the wine," he chortled, "and two glasses. You hero, Edward!"

I lifted the occasional table, positioned it between us, and poured two generous measures of wine.

"Penny is a dear," he said, sipping the wine and smacking his lips, "but she does rather boss me about. I'm sure the occasional indulgence won't do me any harm, especially at my age."

"I'm sure it won't," I concurred. "In fact, I think it'll do you a power of good."

"I'll drink to that!" he said. "Though I must admit," he went on, "that I passed a rather sleepless night, and I'm not feeling too well today. That's the damnable thing about this condition, you know. I'm so dashed up and down. And the old memory… I can recall what happened thirty years ago as clear as a bell, but the events of last week…? Gone!"

I murmured my commiserations.

"Now, would you mind refreshing my memory? I know I summoned you here for a purpose … and not just to sneak me a bottle of vino."

I smiled. "You mentioned Timothy, and you said you'd tell me about … 'all *that*'."

"All *that*…" he said reflectively, and for a moment, I feared he was about to ask me what "all *that*" might refer to.

"Ah, yes," he said, and took another mouthful of wine.

His gaze seemed distant as he stared into the empty hearth. "Would you say that you are a rationalist, Edward?"

I nodded. "I would, yes," I agreed, wondering where this might be leading.

"But would you agree that a belief in rationalism does not preclude the acceptance of the … the fantastical, let's say?"

I thought about it, then nodded. "I would agree, though only if the fantastical is not occult in origin. Something can be fantastical but explicable, eventually."

"I quite agree with you there, old boy. Now…" he regarded his wine, "I understand that Timothy collared you the other evening, and bent your ear."

I smiled. "You could say that, yes."

"He mentioned the accident, Penny says."

"That's right."

He drained his wine. "If you would be so good as to…" he said, proffering his glass.

I refilled it, and he sat back and rested his head on the antimacassar. "A couple of years ago, Penny kindly let me live at the gatehouse here while I had my house in the village renovated. I was suffering from insomnia at the time, and had taken to going for a wander in the early hours. It was jolly good fortune that I did so on that particular evening. It was the very last day of January, and I was returning to the gatehouse when I heard the screech of brakes followed by the fearful din of the car demolishing the wall. I hurried as fast as I was able and saw the wreckage in the moonlight, and Penny and Timothy lying nearby. Both were injured… I did what I could to minister to their wounds. As luck would have it, just a week earlier Penny had insisted that it would be a good idea if I bought a mobile phone, and keep it in my jacket pocket, and so I was able to call for an ambulance." He patted the breast pocket of his tweed jacket and fell silent.

He gazed at the fireplace, slowly shaking his head. "The accident brought back so many memories."

After another period of silence, I prompted, "Memories?"

He looked up abruptly, as if startled to recall my presence, then nodded and went on, "It wasn't the first time I'd helped the injured," he said, "but I don't expect you to believe a word I'm about to tell you."

I smiled. "Let me be the judge of that."

"Bear in mind what you told me – that you are a rationalist who can accept the fantastical."

I nodded, intrigued. "I'll do that," I promised.

"In that case… I have told no one about what happened, not even Penny. It didn't seem … relevant, and anyway, no one would credit it. I doubt that you will, though I think you have an open mind."

*

Lattimer tells a cracking story of interstellar intrigue with great characters and up-to-the-minute science…

– John Brunner, cover quote for *The Castaways of Canopus* by George Lattimer, DAW Books, 1972

*

"This happened five years ago," Lattimer said, "late one summer's night – my last summer in this house, as it happened. It was getting dark, about ten-thirty, eleven. I was in here, reading, with a bottle of port at my elbow. But I'd not had much to drink, Edward, if that's what you're thinking… Barely a small glass, so I wasn't blotto. Anyway, there I was, enjoying a good book, when I heard an almighty crash, an explosion, just out there…" He pointed towards the rear of the house. "So I jumped up and investigated. Don't know what I expected to find. I thought perhaps the generator had blown up – back then, the manor wasn't on the mains, and I had one to power the electricity. Anyway, out through the French windows I trotted towards a strange greenish glow beyond the box hedge.

"Imagine my consternation when I rounded the hedge and found one of my outbuildings demolished. A pile of bricks, no more, and coming from somewhere among them, this green glow. So I approached the rubble and peered into the luminescence."

I leaned forward. No doubt it sounds to you, as it did to me at the time, like something from one of the paperbacks he'd penned back in the fifties. Despite my innate scepticism, I could tell, from the tone of his voice, and the expression of his face as he relived the events of that night, that he believed absolutely in the truth of what he was telling me.

"What did you see, George?"

He swallowed. A tear trickled from the corner of his eye as he nodded and said in a tiny voice, "Two beings ... two small beings. Not human, but humanoid. About the size of ten-year-old children, and garbed in those one-piece suits so beloved of old-time science-fiction films. It was obvious that they were injured, lying there in the rubble, though conscious and in great distress. I ... I did what I could to help them. One was bleeding badly from a leg wound. I fetched a length of washing line from one of the outbuildings, and fashioned a crude tourniquet. Then I moved on to the second creature. He or she appeared to have suffered a chest injury, and several of its ribs appeared crushed, broken... It was having difficulty breathing, and I gave it mouth to mouth resuscitation..." He shook his head. "I have absolutely no idea if my ministrations did any good at all, but I did what I could, Edward. I did what I could..."

I raised the glass to my lips, but hardly tasted the wine.

He took a breath and continued: "And then what happened next was perhaps the most amazing event of that amazing evening, hard though that might be to believe... As I was bending over the second figure, regaining my breath, only then did I notice the source of the green glow – a strange oval-shaped device about the size of a hand mirror, on the floor a yard or so from the first figure. As I stared at it, the glow seemed to grow brighter, and then expanded…"

He stopped and stared at me, his mouth hanging open; he shook his head. He looked as astounded, I thought, as he must have been all those years ago.

He went on in a wavering voice, "And then … you won't believe me, but I swear … I swear by everything in which I believe … that this is what happened. The light expanded and hung in the air, a great oval perhaps eight feet high, and I could see through that oval, Edward, I could see into … into…" He shook his head. "The interior of a building, a great building, and in that building were hundreds – maybe even thousands – of small beings like the ones that lay nearby. As I stared at the pulsing oval, I saw three of these entities approach from this building, step through the portal … and walk towards me and their injured compatriots. I must admit that I felt a terror I had never known in my life before! Two of the beings approached the injured pair, bent over them, gently picked them up and carried them back through the portal into the otherworldly building. The third … the third figure came across to me… I think I cried out. I was scared, I admit, hardly able to take in what was happening. The being paused, and then reached out a small hand, and…"

My pulse was racing. I stared into his watery eyes as he tried to articulate what had happened next.

"George?" I said.

In barely a whisper, he said: "The creature communicated with me. I heard no words, but the sense of what it thought expanded within my head, and to this very day, I can recall what it was that this strange being 'said' to me. It thanked me for coming to the aid of its brothers – and its thanks were not just words… How can I fully describe just what I felt, then? Somehow, I could sense – *feel* – its gratitude, and that of all its brethren back in the *other world*. Then it said, or somehow communicated the fact, that it was about to make a gift to me – a gift that I could use as I saw fit, to help either myself or others. It reached out and touched my forehead, and I felt a great, wondrous heat pass into my head and suffuse my being, and I felt gloriously uplifted, exalted, as the being stepped back, staring at me with its huge black eyes. I said something, asked it a question, and then another … many questions... Who were they? From where did they come? What were they doing here? Were they alien, or beings from another dimension? And … would they come again?" He shook his head. "But rather than answer me, the third being stepped back through the portal, into the building, and as I watched, the scene faded and the oval shrank, and the green glow diminished and extinguished itself. I … I searched frantically for the device from which the glow had emanated, but of course, it was no longer there."

He fell silent, staring down at his clasped hands.

He smiled at me. "Another glass of wine, I think…"

I refilled his glass, and then mine.

"I soon learned what gift the being had bestowed upon me. A few days later, I was chopping wood when the axe slipped and cut into my shin, gashing it badly. I instinctively I knew what I should do, and placed my hand over the wound. I felt an incredible heat flow down my arm, and the pain gradually abated. As I watched, the gash healed itself." He smiled. "I recall I cracked open a rather good bottle of wine that night. Then, a week or so later… I had a dog, a red setter. I was out in the woods one morning when off he went into the trees after a rabbit, and a minute later, I heard his frantic yelping and batted my way through the undergrowth after him. I found him … a front leg caught in a snare. It was broken, snapped clean through, and he was in terrible pain…"

"And you healed him?"

"I managed to open the accursed trap and free his mangled leg. I held it and felt heat pass from me to him. His breathing became even, and the bone knitted, can you believe, and the flesh healed. Within fifteen minutes, he was walking with me – limping slightly, mind – back home."

I took a long drink of wine, and said, "And when you found Penny and Timothy, after the accident…?"

"First of all, Edward, I must explain that I was aware that every time I used my gift, as I thought of it, I knew that its powers were diminishing. The healing took longer each time, and the effects were not as comprehensively successful. I had to be very careful, and sparing, with how I used the gift…

"When I fell ill, a couple of months after the … the visitation … I faced a dilemma. I could use my powers to effect a cure – but in doing so, I would extinguish the gift and so be unable to help others. So I compromised. I used a little of my powers to ameliorate the worst of my symptoms, but I relied mainly on earthly drugs.

"Then came the night of the accident, and how grateful I was that I had refrained from attempting to wholly cure myself! I found Penny, her skull stove open and her right arm almost wholly severed, close to death… I did what I could, exhausted myself and almost all my powers, and healed her, or did as much as I was able. Then I moved on to Timothy and managed to stem his bleeding … though my powers were almost spent by then, and I could not effect the complete healing of his hand."

"You saved their lives…" I said, incredulous.

He inclined his head. "They were the very last people I was able to assist."

I poured more wine, and we sat in silence for a time and drank.

"You haven't told Penny about any of this?"

He shook his head. "You cannot foresee how some people might take such a fantastical story, nor how she might take the fact that she was dying that night, and that I saved her. I think it might be best, on reflection, to let my secret lie, don't you?"

I agreed with him, and poured more wine. Later, he said that he was tired, and would I assist him to his room?

*

106

I think it high time that George Lattimer is given a Grand Master award.

– Algis Budrys, interviewed in 2005

*

The following morning, still in something of a daze after breakfast, I left the house through the French windows, and approached the ruins where five years ago, according to George Lattimer, he had been visited by strange, otherworldly beings.

I stepped over the tumbled stones and gazed about the debris, then knelt and sifted my fingers through the soil. Buried in the pit, I found a strip of thick rubber and pulled it from the earth. Then I dug a little deeper and came across a twisted shard of metal perhaps three inches long, and then another. I set these aside and stood, dusting my hands.

I was aware of an odour, and sniffed my fingers: the faint but lingering aroma of petrol.

Could the metal and rubber be from a generator, I asked myself? Was the explosion not the result of a portal opening from another dimension, but more prosaically, the detonation of an overheated mechanism? And had George Lattimer, suffering the terrible effects of his disease, simply imagined the meeting between himself and the emissaries from elsewhere?

I recalled what Timothy had told me the other night about the scene of the accident in the lane being suffused with an eerie glow, and returned to the library.

Lattimer had said that the crash occurred on the very last day of January, and I googled the date and found what I wanted to know. Then I left the house and made my way to the village.

Laurel House stood amid elm and beech trees in a big garden adjacent to the church. I stepped diffidently through the porch, and encountered a smiling grey-haired lady in the tiled hallway. "I was wondering if Timothy is still…?"

"Ah, Mr Grainger. Yes, he's taking tea in the garden, if you'd care to go through."

I thanked her, and following her directions, made my way down a chess-tiled corridor to an open back door. A lawn flanked by laurel and cherry trees slumbered in the morning sunlight.

The young man was sitting at a circular table with his back to me, sipping from a china cup. I crossed the lawn and apologised for disturbing his breakfast.

He appeared uneasy at my presence and smiled diffidently. "Mr Bentley..."

I pulled a heavy cast-iron chair from the table and sat down. "The other night. I was drunk. I said I'd like to talk, once I'd sobered up."

He looked away from me, as if embarrassed. "That's right, you did."

I gestured. "What you're doing is helping no one, you know? It certainly isn't helping Penny, and I've no doubt that you're gaining nothing. Quite the opposite, in fact..."

"Do you know what it's like to love someone," he said, "and not to have that love returned?"

"I'm almost sixty," I said, smiling. "Of course I do."

"And what makes the pain even harder to bear, Mr Bentley, is that I had Penny, and it was my own stupid fault that I lost her."

"I'm sorry," I said. "Sometimes..." I groped around for the right words, "sometimes we just have to know when it's wise to let go."

"That's easy for you to say," he snapped. "What the hell have you ever lost?"

I sat in silence for a time, listening to the birdsong.

"Well..." I said. "Where to begin? Three months ago my wife left me, and twenty-five years ago..." I stopped, not sure that I wanted to go there, or even begin to suggest that there was a comparison between Timothy's loss and my own.

"All those years ago," I said, "my daughter died. She was six months old. It was a hellish time, but ... but you carry on. You survive. You know, the cliché is correct: experiencing something

108

like that can make you stronger. Alternatively, you can let it corrode you. As I did."

He glanced at me, almost suspiciously.

I went on, quietly. "I found the pain too much. I was reluctant to … to try again, though my wife wanted children. I talked her round, in the end. But I shouldn't have, I see now. I denied her something special, and she resented me. And I'll have that on my conscience forever."

"I thought you said it made you stronger?" he almost sneered.

I considered his words. "Perhaps it did," I said, "but it took me a long time to realise the fool I'd been. One day, Timothy, you'll look back and realise that what you're doing here, what you're putting Penny through, is a mistake, and damaging for both of you. And you'll regret your actions. Please … accept that what you had with Penny is over, and move on."

"And leave her to that Lattimer character?"

I stared at him, recalling something he'd said in the lane the other evening. "You said you resented the hold he had over her," I said. "What did you mean by that?"

He shrugged, looked away. "The way she fusses over him, it's almost as if she reveres him – "

"Lattimer is the father she never had," I told him. "Well, she had a father, but in name only. They were never close. You shouldn't resent her for what she needs."

He stared sullenly at the grass.

I paused, considering my words, then asked, "That night, the night of the accident … what did you see?"

He looked up at me. "See?"

"You mentioned a light, an odd glow…"

He sighed and shook his head. "I don't know. I was delirious, passing in and out of consciousness. I saw the figure – Lattimer, it turned out – bathed in light." He frowned to himself.

109

"It was a full moon," I said. "I checked. And the light of the moon, on the frosted ground... Do you think it was that?" I wonder if he noticed the eagerness in my tone.

His brow furrowed as he thought back. At last he shook his head. "No, that is ... I really don't know. It seems so long ago."

"But it *might* have been the moonlight?" I pressed.

"Well, I suppose it might. But the thing is, at the time, I was convinced that it wasn't."

He finished his tea and said that he really must go and pack, as he was returning to Leeds later that morning.

I laid a restraining hand on his arm as he rose to leave.

"Timothy, please remember what I said about regretting your actions."

He stood very still for a second or two, then nodded and made his way inside.

*

It's a happy truth that, occasionally, we can gain by writing about loss.

– From Ed Bentley's speech on accepting the 2008 BSFA best novel award for *Martian Equatorial*

*

Over the course of the next week, as I worked on the second draft of the novel, George Lattimer slowly faded away.

We took to dining together in his study, as if we knew his days were few and that we had to make the most of the time remaining. Though Lattimer hardly touched his food, he defied his nurses' injunctions to forego alcohol, and joined us when we opened a bottle of red. His spirits were high, notwithstanding his visible physical decline – he'd lost weight, and his hand shook terribly as he lifted his glass – and he regaled us with stories of his past: his meeting with the great and the good of the literary world, his travels around Europe and America.

Then one evening towards the end of July, as I was reading through what I'd written that day, one of Lattimer's nurses rushed into the library. "Mr Bentley! It's George – I think you'd better come..."

Fearing the worst, I said, "Fetch Penny – she'll be in her room."

I hurried to Lattimer's bedroom in the east wing, knocked and entered.

The old writer lay in bed, propped up on pillows, looking every one of his ninety-seven years. He smiled as I rushed to his side and pulled up a chair.

Penny entered, the nurse speaking to her in quick whispers. Penny nodded, and sat beside him, across the bed from me. The nurse gave the old man a pill and a glass of water, and left the room.

"It's sunny outside," Lattimer said, staring through the window at the brilliant sunset. "Quite beautiful... Do you know," he went on, his voice almost inaudible, "I really don't mind dying on a day like today."

Penny shook her head. "Don't talk silly, George. You're not going to die..."

"I have nothing to fear, my child. I have led a wondrous life. The things I have seen. Oh, you wouldn't believe it... The wonders! The marvels! I have been so very lucky."

Penny looked across at me, smiling bravely.

"Do you know what I'd like, Penny?" Lattimer asked. "I know it's naughty, and nursey wouldn't approve... But would you do an old man a great favour, and nip along to my study and fetch the port? I think I'd like one last glass or two, you know?"

She nodded. "Of course I will."

I was about to stand and say, "I'll get it," but Lattimer applied pressure on my hand and moved his head minimally to halt me.

As Penny hurried from the room, he said, "We need to talk, Edward, just you and me. We don't have long."

"Talk?" I repeated stupidly.

"It was no coincidence, you know?"

"I'm sorry… What wasn't?"

"Your coming here. I arranged it." He smiled, almost mischievously. "I'd read all your books, you see, every one of them. I could see, from the best… I could tell what kind of man you were. They are a measure of your humanity, Edward, your compassion. I knew you were the man…"

I said, "The book, the collaboration…?"

"It came to me after Penny collaborated with Guy Lincoln. I suggested she find an SF writer with whom to work, and guided her in your direction. She'd read your novels, admired them."

"The novel – you helped her."

He smiled. "I gave her the initial idea, but my writing days were over. That first draft was all Penny's work. I suggested she contact your agent…"

I shook my head. "But why?"

His smile trembled. "I … I want you to ensure that Penny is looked after. You see, she needs someone – someone to…"

I was about to say, "Of course," when the door opened and Penny entered the bedroom carrying the bottle of port and three glasses.

For the next couple of hours, we drank as the sun went down, and Penny talked about the song she was writing and said, "It's for you, George. It's almost finished. I'll play it for you, tomorrow…"

Lattimer smiled. "I'd like that, Penny. I'd like nothing more."

He never did hear the song that Penny had dedicated to him. As midnight approached and moonlight filled the room, his fingers lost their grip on the glass, and his breathing became evermore shallow, and we leant close to him and held his hands.

In the early hours of the morning, George Lattimer passed away peacefully.

*

George Lattimer was a special person, and leaves behind him a legacy of novels and stories which will delight and entertain for years and years to come.

– Ed Bentley, at George Lattimer's memorial service, August 2018

*

His funeral, a week later, was well attended. It seemed that the entire population of Allenby Wold turned out for the event, along with a sprinkling of old faces from the London literary scene. I recognised retired editors, a writer or two, and George's former agent.

I was at Penny's side during the service in the church, and at the grave as the coffin was lowered into the ground.

Later, we left the graveyard and made the short walk to the Knotted Oak.

Penny hesitated. "I'm not sure I'd be welcome," she murmured.

I'd had a word with the landlord when I arranged Lattimer's wake, and in the circumstances he could hardly object to lifting Penny's ban.

"It'll be fine," I said, and led her into the beer garden.

We drank to the memory of George Lattimer; we circulated, and I introduced Penny to his agent and the editors and writers who'd made the long journey from London.

We talked about his work, the fantastical tales he'd told throughout a writing life spanning more than sixty years, and I considered the very last fantastical story he'd told.

As the mourners left the Knotted Oak, or made their way inside, Penny and I remained in the garden. The sun was going down, laying streaks of magenta and argent above the elms, and we sat at a rickety table and talked.

"I'll miss him," she said in a small voice. "The house... It's so big, and it'll seem so empty without George."

"You'll stay on there?"

"Of course," she said, then fell silent. We sipped our drinks.

She looked up. "Ace Doubles," she murmured. "We get on well, don't we, you and me? We make a good team?"

I nodded. "We certainly do."

"So…" She swallowed, then said in a rush, "I've enjoyed the past few weeks, working with you, being with you. Look, the novel needn't be the last. I have ideas… We could write more together. What I'm trying to say is…"

I smiled across the table at her.

She gathered herself. "I don't want to live alone. You could … you could move up here, live at the manor. There's plenty of room. And there's the pub… You like the pub, don't you?"

I reached across the table and took her hand.

"I'm sorry," she said, "I'm being silly and stupid. I know you don't want to leave London."

We sat in silence for a while as the sun went down.

APPENDIX I

Lattimer, George (1921–2018) UK science fiction writer who began his career in the late 1930s, producing work for a variety of American pulp magazines. He published hundreds of pseudonymous short stories, across many genres, before using his own name on a series of interstellar adventure stories for *Amazing Stories, Astounding Science-Fiction,* and later *Galaxy Science Fiction.* In the 1950s, he began writing science fiction at novel length, principally for Ace Books. Between 1955 and 1968, he produced 23 action adventure novels for Ace. These were characterised by swift narrative exposition, complex plots, and an unusual attention to characterisation for the time. The best of these books are the *Time Police* series, comprising *Agent in Time* (1956), *Adrift in the Cambrian* (1957) and *Mission to 3000 AD* (1957). In 1960, Lattimer began a long-running series of novels featuring Ted Freeman, captain of the starship *Pride of Terra,* an exploration ship charting new territory on the rim of the galaxy. These fast-paced adventures, featuring an inventive cast of alien characters and exotic worlds, proved extremely popular with fans and ran to 35 volumes. All his books were reprinted in his native Britain, often rewritten and expanded. When he ceased writing for DAW Books in the mid-1980s, Lattimer produced a dozen paperback originals that appeared in the UK from NEL, Sphere, and latterly, Pan. From this period, his ambitious dystopia, *A Fearful Tomorrow* (1981), was nominated for a Hugo award. Also of note was the time-travel novel, *Yesterday's Man* (1998). His last novel was *Voyage to Vega* (2008), a glorious over-the-top homage to pulp era SF. Lattimer lived all his life in his native Yorkshire, and leaves a legacy of over 80 novels, the best of which show a passionate concern for serious, character-driven story-telling.

APPENDIX II

Cotton, Tuppence Amy (1993–) UK singer-songwriter who was born in Manchester, and attended Newall Green secondary school, Wythenshawe, and studied art at Loughborough University. She sprang to prominence in 2012 with a series of YouTube posts in which she performed her own haunting compositions and talked about her life, her openness and honesty striking a chord with youth in Britain and America. In 2013, she signed a lucrative recording contract with EMI and released her first album, *Wode and Wold*. Her second, *Life in Time*, became a huge hit, as did her follow-up, *Summer Pastorale*. An intensely private person, despite her YouTube popularity, Cotton lives in the North Yorkshire countryside, and lists her hobbies as looking after animals, song-writing and cooking.

APPENDIX III

Bentley, Edward (1960–), UK science-fiction writer who began writing short stories for *Interzone* in the late 1980s, and was soon producing novels that found a faithful, if limited, audience. The best of his early output include the *Calcutta Trilogy* (1990–1992) set in India in 2090, and the stand-alone novels *Capricorn Days* (1996) and *Telepath Blues* (1998). Bentley was never a bestseller, perhaps because his novels refuse to conform to genre expectations in that they eschew the mechanics of hard SF, and tend towards a romanticism that often borders dangerously on the sentimental. However, his 2007 novel *Spiral* did prove popular, selling over 50,000 copies in the UK and US combined. For the past 15 years, Bentley has lived in the village of Allenby Wold, North Yorkshire, and has collaborated with the singer-songwriter Tuppy Cotton on more than a dozen novels.

Eric Brown has never been a New York Times best-selling writer. He has never attended a Clarion SF workshop. He doesn't hold a belt of any colour in any of the martial arts, and he's never been a Navy SEAL. He doesn't live in Seattle.

But Eric Brown *has* won the British Science Fiction Award twice for his short stories, and his novel *Helix Wars* was shortlisted for the 2012 Philip K. Dick award.

Other books by Eric Brown include:

The Kings of Eternity

Kethani

Starship Seasons

Buying Time

Murder Served Cold

The Serene Invasion

There are over 70 more to enjoy.

His latest books include *The Martian Menace*, and the crime novels *Murder by Numbers* and *Murder at Standing Stone Manor*.

He has been a freelance writer for thirty long, long years and lives near Dunbar in Scotland. His website is: www.ericbrown.co.uk

STONE OWL STORIES

Stone Owl Stories is a quarterly series of novella-length tales of speculative fiction. These attractive, pocket-sized books will feature both established and emerging authors.

Come with us as we travel from the forgotten past to the farthest future, and from the depths of the human soul to the ends of the Earth and beyond.

It's a long story... It's a Stone Owl Story!

www.shorelineofinfinity.com/stoneowlstories

SHORELINE
OF INFINITY

Shoreline of Infinity is a science fiction and fantasy focused publisher and events host based in Edinburgh, Scotland.

As well as a range of science fiction related publications Shoreline of Infinity also publishes a monthly magazine featuring new short stories, poetry, artwork, reviews and articles.

Writers we've published include: Iain M. Banks, Jane Yolen, Nalo Hopkison, Charles Stross, Eric Brown, Ken MacLeod, Ada Palmer, Gary Gibson, Jeannette Ng, Adam Roberts, Jo Walton, D. A. Xiaolin Spires, Tim Majors, Pippa Goldschmidt, Zen Cho and Chris Beckett. We're equally proud of all the new writers we've published.

Shoreline of Infinity Science Fiction Magazine received British Fantasy Society Award 2018 for best magazine/periodical.

Shoreline of Infinity also hosts Event Horizon – a monthly live science fiction cabaret in Edinburgh.

To find out more, visit the website:

www.shorelineofinfinity.com

Lightning Source UK Ltd.
Milton Keynes UK
UKHW020629270421
382698UK00006B/286